C000142146

A December
WITH A
Duke

Seductive Scoundrels, Book Three

COLLETTE CAMERON

Blue Rose Romance®

Sweet-to-Spicy Timeless Romance®

A DECEMBER WITH A DUKE
A Sweet Regency Historical Romance
Seductive Scoundrels
Copyright © 2018 Collette Cameron
Cover Design by: Kim Killion

This book is a work of fiction. Names, characters, places, and incidents are the product of the author's imagination or are used fictitiously. Any resemblance to actual events, locales, or persons, living or dead, is coincidental.

All rights reserved under International and Pan-American Copyright Conventions. By downloading or purchasing a print copy of this book, you have been granted the *non*-exclusive, *non*-transferable right to access and read the text of this book.

No part of this text may be reproduced, transmitted, downloaded, decompiled, reverse engineered, or stored in or introduced into any information storage and retrieval system, in any form or by any means, whether electronic or mechanical, now known or hereinafter invented without the express written permission of copyright owner.

Attn: Permissions Coordinator
Blue Rose Romance®
P.O. Box 167, Scappoose, OR 97056

ISBN Paperback: 9781954307575
ISBN eBook: 9781954307568
www.collettecameron.com

"Everleigh?"

Very slowly and just as gently, he placed a bent finger beneath her chin and edged it upward.

"Are you afraid of me?"

Seductive Scoundrels
A Diamond for a Duke
Only a Duke Would Dare
A December with a Duke
What Would a Duke Do?
Wooed by a Wicked Duke
Duchess of His Heart
Never Dance with a Duke
Earl of Wainthorpe
Earl of Scarborough
Wedding her Christmas Duke
The Debutante and the Duke
Earl of Keyworth
Loved by a Dangerous Duke
How to Win a Duke's Heart
When a Duke Desires a Lass

Check out Collette's Other Series
Daughters of Desire (Scandalous Ladies)
Highland Heather Romancing a Scot
The Blue Rose Regency Romances:
The Culpepper Misses
Castle Brides
The Honorable Rogues®
Heart of a Scot

Collections
Lords in Love
Heart of a Scot Books 1-3
The Honorable Rogues® Books 1-3
The Honorable Rogues® Books 4-6
Seductive Scoundrels Series Books 1-3
Seductive Scoundrels Series Books 4-6
The Blue Rose Regency Romances-
The Culpepper Misses Series 1-2

Dedication

For every mother who has lost a beloved child.

Acknowledgements

My VIP Reader group, Collette's Chéris, came through once more and helped me select names for some of the characters in A DECEMBER WITH A DUKE. What would I do without you?

09 December 1809

Ridgewood Court, Essex England

A chorus of laughter spilled from the drawing room, the gaiety echoing down the gleaming marble-floored corridor. The jollity neither enticed Everleigh nor piqued her interest. A hand resting on the banister and her foot poised on the bottom riser, she slanted her head, listening.

That did not sound like the small, intimate gathering Theadosia, Duchess of Sutcliffe, had promised for the nearly month-long house party.

Only close friends and family had been invited,

Thea had assured her when she cajoled Everleigh into staying at Ridgewood Court rather than going home to nearby Fittledale Park each evening. Probably because she knew full well Everleigh wasn't likely to return every day, if at all.

Thea had vowed there wouldn't be a soul who would make Everleigh feel the least uncomfortable, nor any rapscallions inclined to pursue widowed heiresses almost four-and-twenty years of age.

Only eleven people had gathered for tea this afternoon. Afterward, the men—the Duke of Sutcliffe, three other peers of the realm (all dukes as well) and James Brentwood, Thea's brother—had gone riding.

Not Everleigh's definition of a cozy assembly. Two or three at most fit that description.

Nonetheless, the number was sufferable, for a few days at least. Especially since the other females included her cousins Ophelia and Gabriella Breckensole, as well as her step-niece Rayne Westbrook and Theadosia's sister, Jessica. The other women planning to attend the house party would join them for dinner.

Who else had arrived while Everleigh napped the afternoon and early evening away to ease the megrim still niggling around her temples?

Too much excitement—make that tension caused by her dread of gatherings—inevitably brought a headache on. A dose of powders and a lie-down in a darkened chamber with a cool, damp cloth across her eyes had reduced this one to a dull annoyance. Still, the minor throbbing provided a perfect excuse to retire early should the need arise.

Another burst of laughter erupted—this one mostly masculine chortles.

That boisterous din couldn't be the five men from tea. Precisely how many upper crust chaps had been invited? The same number as females to balance the dinner table?

If so, that likely meant four more strutting peacocks. No doubt pampered and privileged gentlemen with nothing better or more meaningful to do with their time than fritter it away at a house party. Or, as experience had taught her, indulge in a dalliance or two *or three* for the party's endurance.

How many times had she witnessed that very thing during the two miserable years she'd been wife to Arnold Chatterton? How many times had her depraved husband carried on with one shameless gillflurt or another while Everleigh barricaded herself in her bedchamber to escape the vile intentions of the other debauchees in attendance?

A shiver juddered across her shoulders, and she firmed her mouth and gave a little shake of her head.

Chatterton was dead.

He had been for almost two years.

He couldn't hurt her anymore.

Neither could his son.

In any event, Theadosia, the daughter of a reverend, wouldn't tolerate those sorts of shenanigans beneath her roof. But how was Thea to know who prowled about in the middle of the night, or what fiend might waylay and force themselves on an unsuspecting lady?

Would all the guests remain until Christmastide?

Boxing Day?

Twelfth Night?

If so, Everleigh assuredly would not.

She enjoyed her solitude too much, hence her turreted bedchamber at Ridgewood, specifically selected for its privacy and isolation from the rest of the guests. Only two other bedchambers and the nursery lay in that wing—all blessedly unoccupied. At least they had been when she'd made her way to her room this afternoon.

She'd heard nothing on her way down to dinner to suggest otherwise.

Descending the last stair, she wrapped her lace shawl closer around her shoulders and weighed her options. She could return to her chamber and request a carriage to take her home. She didn't care that doing so would advance her reputation for icy aloofness. But it would also hurt Theadosia's feelings, and *that* Everleigh did care about.

A great deal, truth to tell.

Theadosia was one of the few people who hadn't judged her, who had remained a true friend.

On the other hand, Everleigh could muster her courage and see who'd arrived and then decide whether to escape. Waylaying a footman and asking him to reel off the names of the guests probably wasn't a good idea, though of the choices, it held the most appeal.

Confound Thea, *the compassionate, meddling wretch,* for her tender heart and ongoing efforts to entice Everleigh into Society again. Drat Thea's determination to help Everleigh overcome her fears and heal. And above all, a pox on her hints that Everleigh should consider allowing suitors to call upon her.

Even—*God forbid*!—contemplate marriage once more.

Didn't she want children? Thea had asked kindly.

With all my heart.

But marry? Be leg-shackled again? Under a man's thumb, and her every movement dictated?

No. *No*!

Never. *Ever*. Again.

Everleigh refused to subject herself to *le beau monde's* marriage mart or consider matrimony. Her experiences in those arenas had proved intolerable, and she'd no wish to repeat them.

Some things one never recovered from. But unless a person had lived through that awfulness, they simply couldn't understand, so Theadosia couldn't be faulted for her efforts. Everleigh's wounds mightn't have been physical, but the scars on her soul had all but crippled her ability to feel.

Theadosia and Sutcliffe's union was a love match. How could Thea possibly appreciate Everleigh's aversion to marriage?

To men?

Or her immense dislike of December?

How she loathed the month.

She'd first met the aging banker, Arnold Chatterton, and his son Frederick at a Christmastide ball four years ago. After following her and generally making a nuisance of himself the better part of the evening, Frederick had come upon her unawares when she'd naively stepped outside for a breath of fresh air. He'd dragged her into the hothouse and forced himself upon her.

Then the sod had bragged to his father about his

conquest, destroying any hope she had of salvaging her reputation by keeping silent about the despoiling. Seems deflowering innocents was a perverse game with them.

Arnold, the old reprobate, seized his chance to gain a young wife and offered her marriage and a settlement to keep the tale quiet. She'd refused at first, but in February, she'd wed him. Seven months later, she gave birth to a darling baby girl, only to lose precious Meredith a fortnight before Christmas that same year.

Arnold still insisted she host all manner of reprobates and degenerates for the Yuletide holiday and the following year as well. In all that time, Everleigh didn't see her cousins or friends for fear they'd meet the same fate she had at either Arnold or Frederick's hands.

But after Meredith died, Everleigh wrote her mother and confessed all. She'd written Ophelia, Gabriella, and Theadosia too, bribing a sympathetic milliner with a pair of kid gloves to post the letters for her.

That January, Arnold and Frederick, two drunken sots on their way home from whatever foul company they'd kept that evening, had been robbed and shot multiple times. They'd both died.

Everleigh hadn't cried a single tear.

Nor did she smile when the will was read, and as Chatterton's closest living kin, she was left his entire fortune. She'd give it all up, every last penny, if Meredith had lived.

Mama too. She'd died from consumption in March of that awful year.

"Mrs. Chatterton, are you lost? May I direct you to the drawing room?"

She started and clutched a hand to the base of her throat, her pulse jumping against her fingertips. A familiar surge of fear-induced adrenaline zipped through her veins. She'd been so lost in her reverie she hadn't heard the blond Adonis masquerading as a footman approach.

He smiled, male appreciation gleaming in his eyes.

That look she knew well. She didn't recognize

him from her other visits. He must be new to his profession, else he'd have learned to conceal his inclinations better.

"I am Hampton." He splayed a snowy white glove against his puffed-out chest. "May I be of service?"

The way he lowered his voice when he said service suggested he offered her something other than directions.

"No."

She shook her head and glanced downward, skewing her lips slightly at her subdued cream gown, trimmed in black and pansy. Perhaps she should've worn the violet bombazine. That frock boasted a higher bodice and didn't flatter her coloring as much as this one did.

"I was just erecting my ramparts and fortifying my buttresses before entering the fray," she said.

"You're wrecking . . . what?"

His handsome face contorted in puzzlement.

Hampton might possess a god's physique and sculpted facial features, but the gorgeous chap was dumb as mud.

"Never mind." She gathered her skirts while pointing down the passageway. "It's along there. Third door. Right?"

"No, the drawing room is on the left, Mrs. Chatterton."

Because there aren't any doorways on the right side, featherbrain.

She was hard put not to gape at his obtuseness.

"I would be *happy* to escort you." Another rakish smile lit his features.

On second thought, mud might shine brighter than this fellow.

Exasperated by his forwardness, she arched a starchy brow.

"There's no need. I've been here many time before, and I'm certain you've duties to attend to. I shan't keep you from them."

There.

Everleigh had just reminded the impudent chap of his position, and if he wanted to keep it, he'd best stop playing the flirt. Next time, she'd report him to Theadosia. Unlike Everleigh's deceased husband and his philandering cohorts, she didn't dally with servants.

Looking somewhat like a rambunctious puppy who had been scolded for nipping too hard, Hampton inclined his head, and she swept past him.

Bolstering her lagging courage, and with shoulders as rigid as the marble her black silk slippers swished upon with each step, she marched toward the drawing room. She'd rather know whether she'd need to give her regrets to Theadosia and depart for home.

At the doorway, she pressed a palm to her roiling stomach, shut her eyes, and drew in a long, steadying breath.

Compose yourself, Everleigh Lucy Katherine Chatterton.

Swallowing, she forced her eyelids open. She formed her mouth into a self-possessed smile and assumed the cool, standoffish mien that had served her well these past four years.

Blast Arnold Chatterton and his evil spawn for turning her into this creature, hiding her fear behind arctic reserve.

A few steps into the room, she halted, and the

smile curving her lips became brittle.

Thirty or more people attired in evening finery occupied the chairs and settees, as well as every nook and corner. Panic clawed its way up her throat, stealing her breath, and restricting her lungs.

This was a mistake.

She shouldn't have come. Not just to dinner but to Ridgewood Court.

How could she have failed to consider the guests living within a reasonable carriage journey?

Buffleheaded nincompoop.

Too late to turn tail and run now.

Or was it?

Long ago, she'd ceased caring what people thought of her. When she'd been accused of marrying Arnold Chatterton for his immense wealth. Ridiculed for doing so, given his reputation for whore-mongering and other more abhorrent habits. Scorned and shunned because of the vulgar company he kept. Yet those same elitist hypocrites regularly skulked into his bank for loans.

She'd held her head high and never let on how the

whispers, cutting looks, and judgments wore away at what little self-respect she had left.

They didn't know the truth of it.

Most people still didn't, and it would remain that way.

She scanned the room again, noting a few more friends, acquaintances, and neighbors. Not all strangers then. This might be bearable. While married, she'd managed larger, much more raucous crowds many times with no lasting ill effects.

Save her nerves wrought ragged for a week afterward.

Which was one reason she avoided large assemblies.

Her attention snared on a dark-eyed man towering above the others, and his well-formed mouth slid a fraction upward as he acknowledged her regard.

Bother and blast.

The disturbing Duke of Sheffield.

Expression bland, she forced her gaze away even as her stomach toppled over itself in the unnerving manner it did when she sensed a man desired her.

Other women might be flattered, possibly encouraging the beau's interest.

Not she, by juniper.

On a night not so very different than this, just such a man had ruined her. Destroyed her life. Stolen her future.

Oh, she could feign politesse, when necessary, but for the most part, she avoided men, trusting few other than James Brentwood and Victor, the Duke of Sutcliffe.

Mouth firmed, she took in the others present, aware that Sheffield's keen focus never left her. With a little start, she realized her skin didn't crawl with the knowledge. She hadn't considered he'd be here. She ought to have done. After all, he'd been at Theadosia and Sutcliffe's wedding ball.

She dared a covert peek at him.

Eyes hooded, he still stared, but not menacingly.

No, if anything, she'd say he appeared intrigued.

Hadn't she made it clear that night she'd no interest in him?

Or any man, for that matter.

Which is exactly what she'd said to him when he'd asked her to dance for a third time at the ball. Surely, he must've known doing so was outside the bounds.

Or, perchance, he was as dense as mud too. Must be an inherent characteristic of immensely good-looking men. Beauty and brawn but a distinct shortage of brains.

How ironic that beautiful women were often accused of being flighty and lacking in intelligence when she'd met an equal number of attractive men who fit that description.

A moment later, Theadosia, Rayne, and Everleigh's cousins glided up to her, their troubled gazes a contrast to the welcoming smiles framing their mouths. They formed a protective semi-circle around her, their bearing guarded.

Her nape hair lifted.

Her protectors were in full defensive mode.

Why?

"Everleigh, don't tell me you're still in half-mourning? It's been almost two years since Father

Chatterton and Frederick died. Your . . . devotion is *touching*."

Caroline's high-pitched sarcastic drawl rose above the quiet murmuring, succeeding in doing what Frederick's widow intended—drawing every eye to Everleigh.

Mortification fixed her to the Aubusson carpet.

How many of those staring knew her secret shame?

Humiliation burgeoned from her middle, sweeping up her chest and neck, and infused her face with heat.

Swathed in a shockingly immodest carmine-colored gown, Caroline's abundant bosoms were on full display. She lifted a sherry glass to her rouged, smirking lips as she stepped from the shadows where spiders and centipedes and other unpleasant creepy-crawlies were wont to loiter.

Some nerve she had pretending any affection for Arnold. Father Chatterton, indeed. Not once had she addressed her father-in-law half so kindly.

Features stern and expression steely, the Duke of Sheffield folded his arms, and leaning one broad shoulder against the doorframe leading to the music room, regarded Caroline with the same distaste as one might warm elephant dung between one's toes.

Theadosia jutted her chin toward Caroline the merest bit.

At once, her sister Jessica and brother James shifted to block Caroline's view. The Dowager Duchess of Sutcliffe followed their lead. With the distinguished banker, Jerome DuBoise, in tow, she took to the field like a general leading the troops and commandeered Caroline's attention.

Known for flaunting Society's rules, even Caroline didn't dare insult her host's powerful mother and continue to target Everleigh.

Childless and older than Everleigh by fourteen years, Caroline most certainly wasn't grieving. No, she'd tossed off mourning weeds a mere six months after her husband's ill-timed death. The only person who'd loathed Frederick Chatterton more than Everleigh stood across the room enjoying the drama she'd stirred.

"Ignore that witch." Ophelia's overly bright smile

belied her clipped words. "She's still furious you inherited everything."

That wasn't the only reason Caroline despised Everleigh. Few knew why, save those standing around her now and Nicolette Twistleton, who speared Caroline a lethal glance as Nicolette wended her way toward them.

Frederick had delighted in boasting to his wife that he'd sired a child with Everleigh while Caroline remained barren after sixteen years of marriage. His cruelty inflamed her hatred of Everleigh, and she made a point to bare her needle-sharp claws and draw blood at every opportunity. Given they'd lived in the same house until Chatterton died, life had been hellish day in and day out.

Only Rayne's presence had made residing at Keighsdon Hall bearable.

"Why is Caroline here?"

With an expert flick of her wrist, Everleigh splayed her hand-painted lace fan. She cut Theadosia a side-long look. Had she known in advance, her friend would've told her—warned her. Of that, Everleigh had no doubt.

"Surely you understand I cannot stay if she remains, Thea," Everleigh said.

Theadosia presented her back to the drawing room's occupants.

"She arrived with the Moffettes," Thea said, with an apologetic grimace. "I'd forgotten they're distant relations to her, on her mother's side, I believe. They're mortified she imposed upon us. Mr. Moffette admitted he considered trussing her like a goose and stuffing her in the larder when they left. Mrs. Moffette all but told Caroline she wasn't welcome, but the daft woman paid her no mind."

Probably because she'd anticipated seeing Everleigh and couldn't resist inflicting more wounds.

Known for her pleasant temperament, Theadosia pinched her lips together, and a slight scowl wrinkled her forehead. "Given her reputation for histrionics, I feared she might say things better left unsaid and cause an ugly scene if I insisted she leave at once."

"Since Uncle Frederick died, she's been hopping from relation to relation, like a starving flea looking for an ever-fatter dog." Rayne made a rude noise and wrinkled her nose. "She wears her welcome out in a hurry."

Arnold's ward, and a welcome ally against the Chattertons, Rayne had soon become like a sister to Everleigh. After his death, it was only natural the two continue to live together, but at Fittledale Park, the pleasant estate Everleigh purchased outside Colchester. That *other* house, where she'd experienced nothing but misery, was sold and the monies donated to a children's home.

Caroline had nearly had an apoplectic fit when Everleigh turned her out. *Not* penniless, as she deserved—and claimed to all who would listen— however. She'd blown through the five thousand pounds in short order, sold the modest but comfortable house in Kent Everleigh had gifted her, and, henceforth, relied upon the goodwill and generosity of her numerous kind-hearted relatives.

"Thank goodness the Moffettes are off to their daughter's to spend the holiday with their first grandchild." Gabriella's hazel eyes rounded in distress, and she sliced a glance over her shoulder. "*She* won't stay on when they leave, will she?"

"Only an utterly gauche bacon-brain would do so." Ophelia—an exact replica of her sister tonight, except she wore the palest blue gown and Gabriella the softest green—also slid Caroline a covert peek.

Nicolette edged nearer, murmuring, "That sounds precisely like something Caroline Chatterton would do. I'm not above shoving her in the lake and hoping she catches lung fever."

Everleigh laid her hand on Theadosia's forearm. "Forgive me, but I'm afraid I'm off as soon as my carriage is readied. I shan't subject myself to that woman's animosity. Two years of her enmity was more than enough."

"No. Please don't go." Theadosia shook her head, her strawberry blonde hair glinting gold in the candlelight. "You are one of my dearest friends, and I so want you to celebrate Christmastide and Twelfth Night with us."

"And your birthday too," Gabriella said, slipping an arm around Everleigh's waist.

Everleigh had hoped thirty-one December might pass without marking her four-and-twentieth birthday.

"Besides, do you have any idea how hard it was to convince Grandfather and Grandmother to allow us to stay at Ridgewood for weeks?" Eyes wide, Gabriella bobbled her head in a silly fashion and grinned at her twin. "When we live but four miles away?"

Ophelia chuckled as she adjusted her glove on her arm. "That did indeed take a great deal of finagling, and they only permitted it if you act as our chaperone. Else we'll have to go home and miss part of the festivities. Grandmama and Grandpapa are ever so stuffy. Why, they snuff the candles at precisely nine o'clock every night."

Poor darlings.

They'd lived with their paternal grandparents since their parents had died of typhoid when they were five. A widow, Everleigh's mother hadn't believed she could provide for them, nor was their room in their modest cottage. Still, the girls had visited one another often.

"Everleigh, you deserve some joy and happiness,"

Nicolette said, and the others agreed with overly bright, encouraging smiles and nods.

"I shall make it clear to Caroline she is not invited for the duration. I don't care if that's unchristian or impolite. She's just mean-spirited and will put a damper on the house party." Theadosia regally inclined her head toward the butler.

Grover acknowledged the sign with an equally noble dip of his chin before leaving the room.

Everleigh must've been the last to arrive downstairs. Now dinner could be served.

Theadosia touched Everleigh's elbow. "I understand if you'd rather a tray was brought to your room tonight, but please don't leave. I have ever so many wonderful things planned for the yuletide. I don't want you to spend it alone again and . . ."

She glanced round the circle of women, then took Everleigh's hand in hers. "And . . . we know what day tomorrow is, dearest."

The day Meredith had died.

Tears blurred Everleigh's vision, and she dropped her gaze to her hand clutching the fan.

"I shouldn't have come. I'll only dampen everyone's spirits with my doldrums."

"Nonsense, darling." Nicolette hugged Everleigh. "We only all agreed to inundate Thea and Sutcliffe for weeks because we care so much for you."

Despite her shameful past, her friends loved her. "Thank you, but I'm just not—"

"Papa?"

A child's frightened voice called out.

Everleigh, along with her friends, swung their heads toward the doorway.

"Papa?" Sobbing echoed in the corridor.

"I want my Pa-pa!"

2

At once, Griffin straightened, bent on preventing one of Sarah's shrieking tantrums.

Why wasn't she asleep?

Another nightmare?

What was she doing out of the nursery?

And how the devil had she managed the stairs and not become lost?

He'd barely found his way to the drawing room this evening. But then again, though he'd been friends with Sutcliffe for years, Griffin had only stayed here once before at Sutcliffe's wedding ball.

That was also the first time he'd laid eyes on the Ice Queen, Everleigh Chatterton.

Even her unique name appealed in a way that made no logical sense.

By all that was holy, she was exquisite tonight.

From her intricately styled gardenia-white hair to her eyes—the arresting green of the Scottish Highlands in spring—and her soft raspberry pink mouth pressed into a severe line at the moment. Her milky gown, trimmed in muted black lace and purple velvet, emphasized her figure but still cloaked her in modesty. She was, in short, a brilliant white diamond amongst vivid gemstones.

He'd no business noting those particulars about her.

Sutcliffe, Pennington, and Bainbridge had made it brutally clear; Mrs. Everleigh Chatterton was not on the market. Would never be if her avowals could be believed.

Griffin, however, *was* on the marriage auction block.

Sarah needed a mother. But not just any mother. She must be a warm, tender-hearted woman who'd accept and love the child as her own. One who didn't care a whit about Sarah's origins. That had proved much harder to achieve than he'd anticipated.

That was why he'd attended dozens of balls, soirées, and musicales, the theater and opera, and house party after house party these past months, seeking the perfect duchess.

He couldn't drag Sarah about with him forever. Regardless, until he had a duchess to look after her, he wouldn't leave her when he traveled, sometimes for months. He had no plans to cease his explorations and voyages until well into his dotage, so a wife had become essential. His hosts knew in advance if they wanted him present, Sarah and Nurse must accompany him. Sarah had suffered enough trauma in her young life.

"Papa?"

Attired in her nightclothes, cute pink toes peeking from beneath her gown and her riot of untamed sable curls falling over her shoulders, the ebony-eyed child toddled into the drawing room, clutching a one-eyed, almost bald raggedy excuse for a doll. A pathetic memento from her former life.

"Papa?"

He maneuvered around a settee, but the expression of utter delight blooming across Everleigh Chatterton's face hitched his step.

Squatting to Sarah's level, she gave a gentle closed-mouth smile and held out her arms.

"Who is your papa, darling? I shall help you find him."

Not so frigid after all.

Or was it just him she disliked?

Griffin braced himself for Sarah's wail of outrage upon having a stranger speak to her, let alone attempt to touch her. In the year the almost three-year-old had lived with him, he still hadn't quite grown accustomed to her spine-scraping vocal outbursts.

Thank God they'd become less frequent. Those first few weeks, his ears rang even in his sleep, such were the force of Sarah's screams.

Instead of screeching at the top of her lungs, Sarah tottered into Mrs. Chatterton's arms.

His jaw came unhinged for an instant, and something behind his ribs wobbled.

Sarah touched the shimmering platinum curls framing Mrs. Chatterton's face.

Rather than get annoyed at having her coiffeur mussed, wonderment widened Everleigh Chatterton's pretty smile.

"Are you an angel?"

Starry-eyed and breathless with awe, Sarah gently fingered an iridescent snowy curl.

After being introduced to Everleigh Chatterton last summer, Griffin had asked his Uncle Jerome DuBoise about the entrancing widow who wouldn't set foot in London and barely spoke to men. Chatterton had been one of Uncle's competitors, and there'd been no love lost between them, yet Uncle had been remarkably guarded in what he revealed about the widow.

Head canted, a bent finger against his mouth, Griffin observed her interacting with Sarah.

Had Everleigh Chatterton married her elderly banker husband for his money, then had an affair with his son as the tattle-mongers whispered? Had the Chatterton men's shootings truly been a robbery gone wrong or actually assassinations as a few still dared to conjecture?

"Nurse says angels have white hair." A fragile, sad smile tilted Sarah's little mouth. "My mamma lives in heaven. Her name is Meera. Have you seen her?"

"Hardly an angel." Caroline Chatterton's nasty muffled laugh lanced through the air. "More like a soiled dove."

How dare *that* immoral hellcat cast dispersions on Everleigh?

Uncle had also shared some unsavory tidbits about the other Mrs. Chatterton. Of course, Griffin had no way of knowing she'd be here tonight or that he'd have the misfortune of meeting her. That was an unlucky coincidence.

In two strides, he was beside her.

"That's beyond enough, Mrs. Chatterton. I'll remind you an innocent child is present."

"So I see, though why some nitwit presumed it appropriate to bring what is obviously some sort of half-breed by-blow to an exclusive *ton* gathering does boggle the mind, does it not?"

Caroline Chatterton arched her back, thrusting her

barely clad bosoms ceilingward as she cast her sultry glance around the room.

If that was for his benefit, she'd wasted her time. He preferred women who didn't feel the need to blatantly display their wares.

Expression coy, she ran her finger around the rim of her glass. "Whose brat do you suppose she is?"

"Mine."

Her jaw sagged. The rouge on her cheeks standing out like candy stripes against her ashen face, her chagrinned gaze darted here and there.

Her bigotry inflamed Griffin's fury. Rage tunneled hotly through his veins, but he casually adjusted a cuff link.

"Which means, Mrs. Chatterton, that half-breed urchin brat outranks *you*."

Caroline's mouth snapped shut, and after she speared him a murderous glare, she stalked off.

James Brentwood chuckled and spoke quietly into Griffin's ear.

"God save the King, hail Mary, and hallelujah. Someone has finally rendered the sluttish shrew mute.

Now if you could please find a way to encourage her departure . . .?"

"Good riddance," the Dowager Duchess said with a satisfied nod. "The only nitwit present tonight just flounced away."

"Hear, hear," Uncle Jerome agreed. "Not a pleasant sort at all. None of the Chatterton's were. Except that one." He slanted his head toward Everleigh. "There's more to being a lady than breeding, and Everleigh Chatterton is quality through and through."

Everleigh stood straight, then rested Sarah on her hip. Her black lace shawl slipped off, exposing a gently sloping ivory shoulder. She shifted Sarah to one arm, and gathering the folds of the shawl, tugged it off.

The Duchess of Sutcliffe stepped forward and accepted it from her.

The ladies who'd swooped in to protect Everleigh Chatterton when she'd arrived exchanged covert glances, their expressions a mixture of compassion and concern.

Sarah promptly laid her cheek against Mrs.

Chatterton's chest, stuffed her thumb in her mouth, and began twirling a strand of hair with her other hand.

It was Griffin's turn to gawk like a country bumpkin come to Town for the first time.

Sarah was not a docile child.

What spell had the Ice Queen cast over the minx?

Everleigh's clear bottle-green gaze roved over the guests, no doubt searching for the child's father.

Face flushed, Nurse scurried into the room a few moments later. "I beg your pardon, Your Grace."

Ten noble heads swiveled toward the door.

"Oh, dear me. So many dukes." She choked on a giggle as she fanned her face with her hand. "I meant the Duke of Sheffield, if you please."

Even more flustered, she twisted her apron, her rounded cheeks candy-apple red.

"Ten dukes under the same roof for weeks." The dowager chuckled as she slowly scrutinized the guests. "I suggest when we're gathered, we address their graces by their titles to avoid further confusion."

A few others murmured their agreement.

Uncle Jerome tucked her hand into his elbow,

beaming down at her as if she'd solved world poverty. "Excellent idea."

She colored prettily under his praise.

If Griffin wasn't mistaken, his uncle would propose to the dowager before year's end. They were well-matched, and he expected she'd accept.

Would that Everleigh Chatterton was similarly minded, but *le bon ton* knew the Ice Queen viewed marriage with the same favor as simultaneously acquiring the pox and the clap.

Griffin made his way to where she held a drowsy Sarah.

Mrs. Chatterton's winged brows arched high, and her pretty eyes fringed with gold-tipped lashes rounded when she realized whose child she held.

"I'm sorry, Your Grace." Her face rosy from exertion and chagrin, Nurse gave Sarah a fond look as she dipped into a clumsy curtsy.

"Little Miss was having trouble going to sleep. I brought her below, and we had a cup of warm, honey-sweetened milk in the breakfast room. With all the extra people in the house, I didn't want the staff to put themselves out on our behalf. She must've heard the adults and come in search of you when I returned the cups to the kitchen."

More than likely, Mrs. Schmidt had dozed off again, and Sarah had escaped the kindly woman. He'd need to see to hiring a governess sooner than anticipated. Sarah wasn't an easy child to mind, and Mrs. Schmidt was simply too advanced in age to keep up with her.

"Come, cherub. I'll see you to bed now." He reached for Sarah, but instead of launching herself into his arms as was her habit, she burrowed deeper into Mrs. Chatterton's chest and wrapped a thin arm around her neck.

"No, Papa." She shook her head against Mrs. Chatterton. "I want Angel Lady to tuck me in."

He smoothed a hand over her dark, silky head, vainly trying to tame the curls.

"Darling, we cannot inconvenience Mrs. Chatterton."

"I don't mind." Everleigh's face softened in the way only a mother's does, and she touched a cheek to

Sarah's crown. "Truly."

The Duchess of Sutcliffe's gaze swung between him and Everleigh. "I'll ask Grover to delay serving dinner."

"No, please go ahead, Thea. I'm sure we'll just be a few minutes," Everleigh said.

She met Griffin's eyes, hers almost shy, and in the deepest depths of those pools, he saw an unspoken need.

"Not more than ten," he assured her. It would likely take that long for everyone to be seated. "Mrs. Schmidt, please make sure the nursery is readied. I don't want to delay Mrs. Chatterton's return any longer than necessary."

With another little bob, Mrs. Schmidt scurried from the drawing room.

"Are you sure you don't want me to carry her?"

Griffin spoke quietly into Everleigh's ear as they entered the corridor.

She gave a slight shake of her head as she gazed at the sleepy child nestled against her.

"I don't think she'd approve." A tender smile

curved her mouth. "I'm rather shocked she's taken to me so."

So, by thunder, was he.

A short while later, after pulling a crocheted coverlet over Sarah and tucking it around her shoulder, Everleigh brushed the back of her fingers against the girl's cheek.

"She's so precious. You are very blessed."

Had her voice caught?

Here was the kind of woman he desired for Sarah's mother. A woman who recognized children were gifts to be treasured, no matter their birth.

"I am indeed."

Forefinger bent, he caressed the sleeping child's satiny cheek too, and he accidentally bumped Everleigh's hand.

An electrical jolt shot to his shoulder and across his chest so strong that it froze him in place for an instant.

Everleigh stiffened and moved away the merest bit, almost fearfully.

"She's adorable when she sleeps but has a

stubborn streak a mile wide when awake." He removed her pathetic stuffed doll with a few remaining strings of dirty black yarn for hair from her clasp. "She doesn't like to be told no."

"I wonder which parent she gets that from?"

The merest hint of sarcasm shaded Everleigh's murmur, and she slid him a teasing sideways glance.

Wonder of wonders.

All it took for the Ice-Queen to thaw was a child.

"Surely you don't mean me?"

Affecting a wounded expression, he held his hand with the doll to his chest.

She rolled a shoulder and stepped away, gazing 'round the quaintly furnished nursery. She appeared wistful. Sad.

"Mrs. Schmidt, Maya's eye is loose again." He handed the nurse the shoddy doll. "Please sew it on tighter. I'm afraid Sarah might choke on it if it came loose."

Mrs. Schmidt *tsked* and *tutted*.

"Of course, sir. I wish the little mite would take to one of the other dolls you've given her. I'm afraid

Maya hasn't many days left in her, and then what will we do?"

"A pox on you for suggesting such an unthinkable thing." His wink belied his words. On a more serious note he added, "Let's hope she doesn't need Maya as much when the time comes."

With a hearty sigh, Mrs. Schmidt sank heavily into an armchair, then examined Maya's frayed seams.

Griffin extended his elbow to Everleigh. "We'd best get ourselves to dinner, Mrs. Chatterton. I wouldn't want to incur the new Duchess of Sutcliffe's wrath for being overly tardy."

After the slightest hesitation, she touched her fingertips to his forearm, and another tremor of awareness coursed through him.

"Theadosia doesn't get angry about things like that. She's one of the kindest people I know. She won't mind that we are late." With a last melancholy glance around the nursery, Everleigh allowed Griffin to escort her from the room.

"How many children do you have, Mrs. Chatterton?"

A look of utter devastation swept her features before she lowered her eyes and withdrew her fingers from his arm.

"None."

"But I thought . . ."

He clamped his teeth together, wracking his brain. How many years had she been married? Hadn't Uncle Jerome mentioned a pregnancy when he spoke of her? Griffin couldn't recall now, but he'd be asking at the first opportunity.

"Forgive me if I caused offense. I assumed you did because of how naturally you took to Sarah and she to you. You have a mother's instincts." Oddly bereft after she withdrew her hand, he tucked his thumb inside his coat's lapel. "She doesn't often let anyone but Nurse and me touch her."

Everleigh tilted her head, her keen gaze roving his face.

"Then I am honored she permitted me to carry her." A ghost of a smile touched her soft mouth. "I always thought I'd have made a good mother."

"You're not too old to have children."

She couldn't be more than five and twenty, and if Sarah was an example, Everleigh clearly adored children.

A noise very much like a derisive snort escaped her.

"True, but I've no intention of bringing illegitimate offspring into this world and submitting them to that sort of ridicule. Nothing short of Jesus Christ himself appearing with an acceptable man in tow would induce me to ever marry again."

Jerome had mentioned her marriage was a misalliance of monumental proportions. If she had married for money, did she regret her choice? If she hadn't . . .

What other reason could there be for marrying a degenerate nearly old enough to be her grandfather?

Love? Could she have loved the elderly reprobate after all?

"Tell me about your Sarah," Everleigh said. "How old is she?"

They'd made the landing, and Griffin took her elbow as they began the descent. "She's almost three.

In fact, her birthday is the thirty-first of this month."

"So is mine!"

When Everleigh smiled with genuine happiness, joy bloomed across her face, making her even more impossibly lovely. She touched a finger to the onyx and pearl locket resting just below the juncture of her throat and collar bone.

Curse him for a fool.

She wore a mourning locket.

Maybe she really had loved the ancient sod she'd been married to and could overlook his indiscretions and other deplorable vices. Some swore love covered a multitude of sins.

Grief settled over her as tangible and dense as a woolen cloak. "Had she lived, Meredith would've been three last September."

Was he supposed to know who she was?

"Meredith?"

3

For the second time that night, Everleigh stopped on the last riser.

He truly didn't know?

"Yes, my daughter, Meredith."

She touched the locket again. A lock of wispy, thistle-down soft white hair lay tucked inside. Struggling to wrestle her grief into submission, she focused on the long case clock's pendulum swinging back and forth.

She paced her breathing with the slow *tick-tock* for a handful of rhythmic beats.

Did a parent ever recover from the loss of a child?

No. Life just took on a new reality.

"Tomorrow is the third anniversary of her death."

Why had she shared that?

The Duke of Sheffield did the most startling, the most perfect thing in the world.

He drew her into his arms and held her. He didn't offer condolences or advice. He didn't try to change the subject or pretend he hadn't heard her.

He simply offered her comfort, and it felt so utterly splendid, just allowing someone to hold her. Someone who permitted her to show her grief for a child conceived in the worst sort of violation and violence but who had been adored nevertheless.

For this brief interlude, Everleigh didn't have to be strong. Didn't have to maintain her frigid façade, and it was wonderful to be herself. That almost brought her to tears as well.

What was more astonishing was she wasn't afraid of his touch.

How long had it been since she didn't flinch when a man touched her?

They stood chest to chest and thigh to thigh in intimate silence for several moments until the clocked chimed the quarter-hour and interrupted the tranquility. They really must join the others for dinner, or God only knew what sort of unsavory tattle might arise.

"Thank you for your kindness, Your Grace."

She disengaged herself, more aware of him as a man than she'd any business being.

He simply nodded, though the amber starburst in his eyes glowed with a warmth she couldn't identify.

At the bottom of the stairs, he again placed her hand on his forearm and steered her toward the dining room. Evidently, he didn't feel the need to fill the stillness with inane chatter.

She liked that about him. It was fine to speak when something needed to be said, but it was equally acceptable to let silence fill the comfortable void when it didn't. At home, she'd sit with her eyes closed and listen to the quiet, especially in the early morning when the countryside began to wake.

A few minutes later, they entered the dining room. Several people noted their entrance, including Caroline, who raised a superior brow, then murmured something to Major McHugh on her right. The major's wiry gray eyebrows scampered up his broad, furrowed forehead, and skepticism and disapproval jockeyed back and forth for dominance in his acute regard of Everleigh.

Whether by chance or Thea's maneuvering, the two remaining vacant chairs were at opposites ends of the table. Everleigh wasn't certain if she should feel vexed or grateful, but her estimation of the Duke of Sheffield had increased a few degrees this past half hour. Not enough to garner further interest, but she no longer considered him a licentious rake to be avoided at every turn.

An hour and a half later, as the ladies made their way to the drawing room for tea and to play whist while the gentlemen enjoyed their port, she made her excuses to Thea. She'd chew hot coals before enduring Caroline's unpleasant company any longer.

"I'm going to retire early," Everleigh said. "I fear my headache from this afternoon never completely went away."

That was the truth.

Thea took her elbow and drew her aside as the

other ladies filed into the drawing room. Ophelia, Rayne, and Gabriella stopped strategically just beyond Theadosia and Everleigh, blocking the view of any curious eavesdroppers.

Everleigh's heart swelled with gratitude. She truly did have the most marvelous friends.

"You will stay on, won't you, Everleigh?" Thea looked past the trio quietly chatting a few feet away to Caroline seated on a settee and directing a haughty glare toward them. "I promise, she'll be gone before you come down to breakfast if I have to bundle her, tied hand and foot, into the carriage myself."

Pretty doe-like eyes flashed to mind, followed by a black coffee pair set beneath straight brows the same rich shade.

"If Caroline is gone, I'll stay a couple more days. That's all I can promise for now."

Grinning, Thea hugged her.

"Excellent. Tomorrow we'll attend church, of course. It is also Stir-up Day. I want all the guests to stir the Christmas pudding and make a wish. I've charades planned for the evening, along with mulled cider from Ridgewood's very own apples."

Theadosia's eyes twinkled with excitement. "The women will make kissing boughs—mistletoe has been drying for a fortnight, and the gentleman will go stalking. Cook absolutely insists on fresh venison for the Christmas feast. That's just to start the festivities. I've much, much more planned."

Theadosia had always adored Christmas.

"It sounds like a great good"—*exhausting*—"time," Everleigh managed to say without seeming overwhelmed.

It truly did for someone who enjoyed large assemblies and holiday traditions. She preferred a quiet gathering: family, close friends, a Yule log crackling in the hearth, steaming spiced cider, a mistletoe sprig, and perhaps a Twelfth Night Cake.

Another swift perusal of the drawing room revealed Caroline no longer sat on the settee. Maybe she'd crawled back into her hole or rejoined her coven.

One could only hope.

Everleigh bussed Thea's cheek and wiggled her fingers farewell to the others.

"I'll see you in the morning."

Instead of going directly to her chamber, she stopped at the library. Better to keep her mind occupied than let her musings have free rein. Besides, reading always made her drowsy. Tomorrow would prove difficult enough without a sleepless night.

As she perused the shelves, she removed her gloves.

What should she read?

Something entertaining?

Educational?

Or a boring tome?

Once she'd selected one of each type, she continued on her way, shawl over her forearm and her gloves draped over the books. Laughter filtered down the passageway, and she bent her mouth into the merest semblance of a smile. Tonight had been much more pleasant than she'd expected.

Except for Caroline's presence, of course.

As she reached her bedchamber and grasped the door handle, her nemesis emerged from the shadows near the floor-to-ceiling window alcove. She seemed to have a habit of slithering out of dark corners. Caroline held a glass half full of what looked to be brandy, a favorite and common indulgence.

Been raiding Sutcliffe's liquor cabinet, had she?

"It wasn't enough you seduced my husband and persuaded Arnold to wed you to hide the whelp swelling your belly, Everleigh. You managed to manipulate him into changing his will, then turned me out onto the street to starve."

Caroline had merely alluded to those things before. Either drink or fury had emboldened her to speak them outright tonight. Thank God she'd not done so in front of the others.

"Not a single word of that is true, as you well know."

One eye on the nursery three doors down, Everleigh opened her chamber.

Caroline took a long pull from her glass, then, eyes narrowed until they were almost closed, advanced toward Everleigh. She pointed the forefinger of the hand holding the nearly empty glass and fairly hissed, "If it's the last thing I do, I'll make you pay, you cold, unfeeling witch."

"You're drunk, Caroline." Also a frequent occurrence. "Go to bed before you embarrass yourself."

Again.

Caroline stalked nearer, her once pretty face contorted with hatred and showing the ravages of too much drink and other unhealthy indulgences.

"I've heard ugly rumors, Everleigh. Murmurs that someone hired rum pads to kill Arnold and Frederick and make it look like a robbery."

That was the first Everleigh had ever heard any such thing, and the accusation gave her pause as well as sent chilly prickles across her shoulders.

Could such a thing possibly be true?

Wouldn't there have been an inquiry long before this?

Were people, perhaps even those at this gathering, speculating about whether she'd been behind her husband's death?

Everleigh glanced toward the nursery again as she crossed the threshold. "Keep your voice down. Sarah is sleeping a bit farther along the passage."

Even as she spoke, a child's muffled cries echoed.

"Do you think I give a whit about that merry-begotten?" Caroline finished the rest of her brandy and leaned indolently against the wall, the glass dangling from her fingers. "Who, besides you, hated Arnold and Frederick enough to want them dead?"

Any of a dozen people Everleigh could name, including the foxed woman standing before her.

"I've done nothing wrong, and I'll not listen to your vile accusations." No doubt conjured by jealousy and hatred. "I had no knowledge of the attack on Arnold and Frederick until the sheriff delivered the news."

She laid her belongings on the table beside the door, undecided if she should knock at the nursery. It wasn't her place to offer to help with Sarah, but she was partially responsible for the child's sleep being disturbed.

She spared Caroline a brusque glance.

"If the authorities had reason to believe something afoul of the law occurred, they would have investigated already," the Duke of Sheffield said.

Everleigh and Caroline swung their attention to him ambling toward them, all masculine prowess and power. His black evening attire accented the broad span of his shoulders, and the corridor seemed to shrink with his presence.

Everleigh forced her gaze away.

Just because she'd noticed his manliness, it didn't mean anything. She was, after all, still a young woman.

"Unless, Mrs. Chatterton, you know something no one else does?" He cocked his head at a considering angle then rubbed the scar dissecting his slightly bent nose with his forefinger. "But then, you'd have to explain to the authorities why you've withheld information all this time. I believe that's a criminal offense too."

Arching her back, the calculated movement thrusting her chest upward, Caroline stretched like a contented cat. More like an eager-to-be-bred tabby twitching her tail before a tom. She gave him a secretive smile as she glided past and tapped his chest with her empty glass.

"We'll just have to wait and see, won't we?"

She sent a sly look behind her, flicking Everleigh a glance that clearly said she found her wanting.

"I do hope you have an alibi, Everleigh."

Mouth pinched, Everleigh stared at Caroline's retreating back.

Was she serious?

Did she truly intend to claim that Everleigh had something to do with the robbery and murders? Surely no one would believe such an assertion at this late date. Nevertheless, her stomach twisted with anxiety.

"Are you all right?" Sheffield also watched Caroline flouncing away. "Did she upset you? You've gone quite pale."

Everleigh sighed and pressed her fingertips to her right temple where the pain had taken on a renewed vigor.

"Caroline delights in upsetting me, but I'm fine."

"Are you sure?" He touched her cheek with a bent knuckle. "The light behind your eyes is gone."

Light behind her eyes?

What nonsensical drivel.

She wouldn't have thought he was the sort to bandy platitudes about.

"Ridiculous. I've but a pesky headache."

Her response was starchier than she'd intended.

He chuckled and swept a strand of hair off his forehead. "No need to get prickly, and I regret you're not feeling well."

"I cannot believe she'd resort to such fabrications simply to hurt me." Everleigh absently rubbed her hairline near her ear.

Judging from the strain of the fabric, he rested what surely must be a well-muscled shoulder against the wall.

"Envy and jealousy can turn even the most decent men into fiends. But when someone is already despicable, there's no telling what they're capable of." He spared a thoughtful glance toward the stairs. "The Duchess tells me Mrs. Chatterton will be gone in the morning. We're well rid of her, but I think you still must be on your guard against her."

Everleigh touched her locket, running her fingers across the diamond floweret atop the jet. "Believe me,

I have been for four years."

"Do you have an alibi? Someone who can vouch for you?"

He seemed genuinely concerned, not just prying.

She sighed and stretched her neck from side to side, hoping to lessen the knots of tension that had taken up residence there.

"My husband kept me a virtual prisoner. I hadn't access to funds to hire someone to commit the foul deed. Even my jewelry was kept locked in a safe, so I couldn't use it to bribe a servant. I rarely left the house, and when I did, two of my husband's henchmen accompanied me to prevent any escape attempt."

Not that she would've tried, for fear Arnold would harm her family as he'd threatened.

"He really was a bloody blighter, wasn't he?"

Disgust and anger riddled the duke's clipped speech.

"He was."

She clasped her hands behind her back, then leaned against the doorjamb.

"The former staff can vouch that I was never

permitted personal visitors, and the only guests we entertained were the miscreants and other dregs of society my husband invited. The night he and Frederick were slain, I was . . ."

She paused, lost in the dreadful memory.

"You were . . .?" his grace prompted with an encouraging closed-mouth smile.

She'd not told anyone about the thrashings.

"Let's just say I was incapable of leaving my bed, and the sheriff can testify to that."

The duke's intense gaze probed hers, and she didn't doubt his mind flipped through numerous scenarios to explain why she would've been abed.

His eyes turned stone-hard, as did the sharp angles of his face.

He'd hit upon the truth. Rather more swiftly than Everleigh would've thought.

"Chatterton beat you?" he said, his voice fury-roughened.

Whenever Arnold tried to copulate and couldn't get his limp member to cooperate. He'd never once been able to bed her—her one small victory. That she wasn't about to tell the duke. Instead, she gave a curt nod.

"That bloody bounder." Posture rigid, Sheffield dropped his balled hands to his sides. "No wonder you're so afraid."

Sarah's fussing continued to carry through the closed nursery door.

Uncomfortable at having shared something so intimate, she scrambled to change the subject.

"I apologize for waking your daughter."

He cupped his nape, giving her a guarded look from beneath hooded lids.

"Actually, Sarah is not my daughter."

4

Early the next morning, a thick velvet-lined mantle over her black and white striped woolen walking dress and redingote, Everleigh rapped on the nursery door.

She dismissed her misgivings.

Surely the duke couldn't object to Sarah taking a walk, particularly if Nurse accompanied them.

Quiet murmurings beyond the thick panel assured her Nurse and Sarah were awake. The door edged open, and a surprised but pleased smile crinkled Nurse's face.

"Mrs. Chatterton. I thought Young Miss and I were the only ones awake at this hour."

Everleigh looked beyond the plump servant to where Sarah sat fully dressed with an oversized pink bow in her hair, playing with her shabby doll.

"I'm an early riser myself. I thought perhaps Sarah would like to take a walk with me. The frost has made lovely patterns in the gardens, and I saw a rabbit and deer from my chamber windows."

Upon hearing Everleigh, Sarah scampered to the nursery door and pulled on Nurse's skirts.

"May I? Please? Maya too?"

Sarah held up the dilapidated rag doll.

"I'm not sure Miss Sarah ought to be outside. She's still not quite accustomed to England's cold weather." Indecision crimped the nurse's mouth.

Other than saying Sarah was orphaned and born in Southern India, the duke hadn't revealed much more about the child he'd taken in. Everleigh hoped to learn more about the fascinating little girl today.

Sheffield had edged up another notch in her estimation too. She'd best be careful, or she might actually admire him, which wouldn't do at all. Admiration could lead to other sentiments. Dangerous sentiments for a widow committed to keeping her independence.

"If I promise not to keep her too long? You can tell me when you think she's had enough, and we'll come in straightaway. I'm certain Sarah would benefit from the fresh air and exercise."

Perhaps it was because Meredith had died on this day, or maybe Sarah had stirred dormant maternal instincts, but in any event, Everleigh couldn't stay away from the child.

Nurse conceded with a nod and a smile. "You've convinced me. It would do the tike good to run about."

Excellent. Mrs. Schmidt wasn't the type of nurse who thought children should march along like miniature soldiers or sit perfectly still for hours on end.

She leaned in and whispered to Everleigh, "Maybe the little mite will take her lie-down without a fuss if she capers about outside a bit."

Hope tinged the tired servant's voice. She was a trifle too advanced in years to be chasing after such an energetic child.

A few minutes later, Everleigh held Sarah's hand

as they stood on the edge of Ridgewood's neat-as-a-pin gardens and watched a doe nibble the green's succulent frost-tipped grasses. A smaller deer, likely her fawn from last spring, sampled a nearby shrubbery.

"Is that her baby?" Sarah asked while rubbing her cold-reddened nose with her bare hand.

Where had her mitten gone?

Everleigh nodded as she searched the ground for the lost mitten. "I think so."

Mrs. Schmidt, her chins tucked deep into the folds of her cloak, looked on with less enthusiasm.

Heavy pewter clouds covered the sky, hiding all evidence of the sun and hinting at a brewing storm. A brisk breeze toyed with the ribbons of Everleigh's and Sarah's bonnets. It was chilly, but not unbearably so. More importantly, no one else had ventured outdoors yet, and the solitude was sheer bliss.

Likely, most guests were either eating or getting ready to attend church services in Colchester. It was expected, which meant a quiet house for a few hours more.

There was a day when she'd have joined them, but

Arnold—spawn of Satan—hadn't allowed her to go, and Everleigh had never started attending after he'd died.

"What goes on here?"

At the sound of the Duke of Sheffield's voice, Sarah whipped around and then, giggling, her little arms wide, ran to him

"Papa!"

His midnight-blue caped greatcoat gave his black hair, visible beneath his hat, a bluish tint. The unrelenting breeze taunted the cape's edges and the hem of Everleigh's cloak.

"Papa, Mrs. Chatterton showed me deers. When we gets inside, she promised me hot choc'late and clodded cream," Sarah finished in a breathless rush.

"Is that so?" He scooped her into his arms, then whirled her in a circle.

Her delighted screeches frightened the deer away.

He stopped and slung one sturdy arm beneath her thighs. "Did you break your fast already, my pet?"

"Yes, Your Grace." Nurse's kind eyes pleated around the edges in approval. "Little miss had a good appetite this morn. She ate everything but the pickled herring."

"Cannot say that I blame her," Everleigh muttered, then chagrined she'd spoken her thoughts aloud, blushed.

But really?

Pickled fish for breakfast?

She had never been able to appreciate that particular food, let alone breaking one's fast with the smelly little blighters. Almost as revolting as blood sausage, a favorite of Arnold's.

"Well then, that certainly deserves hot chocolate." Amusement sparkling in the duke's eyes, he nuzzled Sarah's cheek, and she giggled again.

"With clodded cream," she reminded him.

"With clotted cream," he agreed solemnly, his gaze seeking Everleigh's over the top of Sarah's head.

His leisurely perusal and the equally unhurried smile bending his mouth upward sent her stomach fluttering. Surely in hunger, for she hadn't eaten yet.

What compelled a man to take an orphan in and treat her as if she were his own? Such a person must be intrinsically decent, mustn't he?

"I hope I didn't overstep." Everleigh drew near and straightened Sarah's rumpled gown and claret-toned coat, then handed her Maya. "I saw the deer from my chamber and thought she'd enjoy seeing them too. I'm afraid they've run off now. We had a lovely walk through the gardens as well."

Sarah nodded, bumping her head on his chin.

"Ow." She clapped a little dimpled hand to her injury.

Everleigh waited for the howl of displeasure, but instead, Sarah took the duke's face between her little palms and insisted he look at her.

"Papa, we sawed a frozen spider web. It looks like Nurse's crotch dollies."

"Oh my." Merriment rounded Mrs. Schmidt's eyes, and shoulder's shaking, she coughed into her glove.

"Crocheted," he gently corrected, his mouth twitching in an effort to contain his mirth. "Nurse crochets doilies."

Everleigh met his eyes, and she almost erupted

into giggles.

"I've always enjoyed an early walk myself, but the breeze grows stiff." He lowered Sarah to the ground. "You go with Nurse now, and Mrs. Chatterton and I shall be along directly. We can all enjoy a cup of chocolate together in the nursery. How does that sound?"

"I want biscuits with my hot choc'late. An' a story too." Sarah scowled at Nurse's outstretched hand.

"Sarah, we ask politely. Please may I have a biscuit and a story with my chocolate?" the duke gently corrected her.

"Yes, Papa." Sarah turned those big eyes to Everleigh. "Please, biscuits an' a story?"

"I'm sure something can be arranged," Everleigh said, keeping her smile under control. It wouldn't do to unravel the duke's effort to teach Sarah manners. "I'll stop by the kitchen and ask. I think I heard the Duchess of Sutcliffe mention gingerbread last night."

"Ginger . . . *bread*?" Her nose crinkling in confusion, Sarah looked between the duke and Everleigh. "I wan' biscuits. Not bread."

"Gingerbread is a kind of biscuit made with . . ." The pleading glance he sent Everleigh silently asking for help warmed her cold toes.

"Molasses, cinnamon, and ginger, and they are shaped like stocky little men." She used to make them with her mother to celebrate the Christmas season. "I like to bite the head off first."

"I wonder why?" The merriment lighting his face revealed he teased her.

"Go along now." He urged Sarah toward Nurse. "And make sure you are agreeable to Mrs. Schmidt, lest I have to deny you your treat."

"I be good, Papa. I promise." Skipping along, her dilapidated doll dragging the ground, Sarah began singing a nonsensical song about chocolate and biscuits and deer.

"She's an absolute darling." Everleigh accepted his extended elbow.

He smiled as he watched her romp away.

"You didn't answer me when I said I hoped I hadn't overstepped, so I presume I did. I should have asked first. Please forgive my forwardness, Your

Grace. I've little experience with children."

Only a few weeks with an infant born healthy but who'd sickened rapidly and died just as swiftly.

He turned back to her and picked a piece of black fuzz from his bent arm.

"You mistake my silence as censure, Mrs. Chatterton. I simply didn't want to speak in front of Sarah. I have no objection to you taking her for an outing. I do have a concern about her growing too attached to you. As I told you last night, she lost her mother under difficult circumstances."

Everleigh swallowed her disappointment and stared at the swaying trees.

He was right, of course.

There was also the danger that she'd grow too attached to Sarah.

"I understand. Please forgive me for not considering that. I was going to ask if we might walk every morning, but I think that might not be wise. In fact, I hadn't decided if I was going to stay for the duration of the party, but given Sarah's reaction to me, I believe it best if I leave directly."

The depths of her distress was startling when yesterday she'd been on the verge of leaving anyway.

Releasing his elbow, she drew her cloak closer as she erected her cool, protective mien. She'd let her guard down, and look where it had landed her?

Tilting her face upward, she inspected the heavens again.

Yes, a storm brewed. Hopefully the clouds didn't portend snow, or Cook mightn't have her stag. Just as well as far as Everleigh was concerned. A fat goose sufficed for Christmas dinner. Let the noble deer live another season.

Snow also meant she'd have a more difficult time getting home. Best to leave straightaway then.

"If you'll excuse me. I need to pack and write Theadosia a note."

She swiveled toward the house, but he touched her shoulder.

"Please don't leave, Everleigh."

His tone compelled her to meet his gaze, and she couldn't look away. The way he'd murmured her name, almost reverently, took her aback. Made her want what could never be. What she'd chosen to forsake for her peace of mind and physical wellbeing.

It—he—wasn't worth the risk.

And yet she still didn't look away from his captivating gaze, the deep russet of his eyes willing her not to break whatever bond linked them at this magical moment.

Foolish, Everleigh!

Haven't you had enough pain for a lifetime?

She toyed with fire, and with a man of his caliber, experienced, and devilish charm, she'd get burned. Charred to cinders.

"What goes on in that beautiful head of yours?" He touched her cheek again, then spread his fingers until they framed her jaw.

Given the temperature, the black leather should've been cool to the touch, yet heat seared her face.

"I see wariness and confusion," he said. "But mostly, dread of being hurt again."

At last, she dropped her gaze to the buttons on his greatcoat. Mouth dry as parchment, she swallowed.

"Why should I stay, Your Grace?"

"Because, Everleigh, I'm inclined to take the risk and grant your request. Sometimes it's necessary to take a chance. Particularly if we seek something worthwhile."

She gave him a hard look.

Was he still talking about Sarah?

Withdrawing his hand, he swept the house a casual glance.

"I've not seen Sarah this animated or cooperative since . . . Well, ever. As I said last night, she hadn't reached her second birthday when I sailed from India with her, and she's had difficulty adjusting. Her reaction to you is nothing short of miraculous."

"She likes my hair." Everleigh raised a hand to her temple. "She says it's angel hair."

"Hair your shade is rare, even in England. She's never seen the like." He gathered her hand and placed it in the crook of his elbow once more.

"You aren't interested in becoming a duchess, are you?"

At once she stiffened and opened her mouth to ring him a peal, but his jovial wink sucked all the ire from her.

He but teased.

"No. Not a duchess or wife to any man of any station ever again."

She couldn't speak plainer. Best to nip in the bud any wayward notions the duke might have. Only a fool didn't learn from past experience.

Rather than taking offense, a sympathetic smile tipped his mouth, and compassion simmered in his dark gaze.

"I admire your pluck. And your strength. You are a remarkable woman, Everleigh Chatterton."

If he'd said he worshipped her beauty or some other flattering hogwash she'd heard before, she'd have been able to dismiss his compliment. Instead, foreign warmth seeped into her bones.

He steered her around an ornate marble fountain topped with a trio of cherubs and four crouching horses beneath. No water flowed today, probably a precaution against the freezing weather.

"Have you eaten yet?" he asked.

"No, I intended to after my walk."

"You don't attend Sunday services in Colchester?"

"No." She shook her head before glancing over her shoulder. A caravan of vehicles rattled and squeaked their way down the drive. "I know it is expected, but I have not been able to go since . . ."

She touched a gloved finger to the oval locket, barely detectable beneath her cloak and redingote.

Would he judge her as so many others had?

She glanced upward, searching his expression for any sign of censure.

"I cannot stop being angry with God for letting Meredith die."

She hadn't been angry with Him after being ruined or forced to wed Arnold. At least not this lingering inability to let go of her hurt. But when she lost her baby too? Well, that had pushed the limits of her faith, and her beliefs had shattered under the weight of her anguish.

Sympathy softened his features. He covered Everleigh's hand with his and squeezed. "You have my sincerest condolences. I cannot fathom the depth of your grief at such a tremendous loss."

"Thank you." She drew in a deep breath, filling her lungs to capacity, willing herself not to cry in front of him. After a second, she released the air in a whoosh.

"Why don't *you* attend church, Your Grace?"

He looked thoughtful for a moment.

"I didn't want to leave Sarah only a day after arriving. True, she mightn't even know I'm gone, but I don't want to put Mrs. Schmidt in that position." He glanced overhead for a long moment. "At one time, I too struggled with anger toward God. When my parents died, but especially after Sarah's mother passed away and she was left an orphan. Time has helped ease that disappointment and a realization that the matter was out of my hands. What I did afterward is what counts."

"You must've loved Sarah's mother very much."

An odd twinge pinched her lungs.

He looked so taken aback that she almost chuckled.

"Meera was a friend, nothing more. Her husband Rajiv saved my life five years ago. I was set upon by thieves. They beat me severely. That's how I got this."

He pointed to his scarred nose.

"But Rajiv chased them off then took me to his house. People here would call it a hovel, but he and Meera had made it into a comfortable home. Though they were poor, they somehow paid for a physician to treat me. They nursed me back to health until I was well enough to tell them who I was. Rajiv refused to let me repay him, though I know he could've used the money."

He stopped and leaned against a Grecian statue.

"Every time I went to India, I visited them. Rajiv wouldn't accept money but allowed me to bring gifts. Sarah's doll is one of them. The time before last, when I arrived, Meera told me Rajiv had died. A bull elephant went berserk and trampled him."

Everleigh sucked in a sharp breath. "That's awful."

A muscle in his jaw flexed.

"Meera and Sarah were on the verge of starvation. I made arrangements to send them funds and supplies monthly since she refused to leave India and come to

England. It was the least I could do."

He grew silent for a moment, his bent forefinger pressed to his lips as if he struggled to control his emotions.

There was more to this man than she'd ever have guessed.

"The last time I was there, I learned that Meera had died. A sickness of some sort. I never did find out what exactly. Another family occupied their house, and Sarah lived in a crate behind it. I don't know why they didn't take her in or if she had any other family, but I knew I must take her from there at once. If I'd been even a week later, she'd have starved to death."

They resumed walking, the frozen gravel crunching beneath their feet.

"The poor little dear."

Tears blurred Everleigh's vision, and she bit the corner of her lower lip against a sob.

Voice husky, she managed, "You are a truly decent man, Your Grace."

He chuckled. "Not everyone would agree with you. I'm no saint, and I don't pretend to be, but common decency demanded I help the child of the man who saved my life."

He mightn't be a saint, but plenty of people wouldn't have thought Sarah their responsibility.

They'd made the house, and he opened the door for her.

"What say you, we have our breakfast in the nursery?" he asked as she stepped inside.

Everleigh grinned for the first time in a long while. "That sounds delightful."

"There you are."

Everleigh went rigid as Caroline's strident voice shattered the pleasant mood.

5

Griffin gnashed his teeth to keep from telling Caroline Chatterton to bugger off.

"I thought you were leaving," he said crisply as he closed the door.

Attired in a dusky green traveling gown, she turned her seductive gaze on him, trailing his form in a manner that made him want to take a bath.

Her rouged mouth twisted slightly to the side.

"I am, just as soon as I've had a word with Everleigh. The carriage awaits me even now. My cousins in Kent are anxious I spend the holiday with them."

Balderdash.

Caroline's cousins probably didn't know she was about to show up on their doorstep and ruin their holiday.

"We don't have anything to say to one another. Please excuse me." Everleigh made to move past her.

"I have a proposition." Caroline played with the fingers of the gloves she held, her arrogance slipping a notch. "I think it would be beneficial to us both, most especially you."

Everleigh sighed but faced her. "What is it?"

"Can we speak privately?" Caroline slid Griffin a pointed glance.

"I'll wait for you in the nursery." He didn't bother lifting his hat in farewell to Caroline.

"I'll be along shortly," Everleigh said. "Don't wait for me to break your fast."

"How positively domesticated you two sound." Jealousy made Caroline's voice strident.

"Should we expect a joyful announcement soon?" She made an exaggerated 'O' with her mouth and pressed two fingers to her lips, feigning surprise. "But I thought you'd sworn off ever marrying again." Her vapid gaze dropped to Everleigh's middle. "Unless . . . you're breeding another illegitimate progeny?"

"Watch your tongue, Mrs. Chatterton." Griffin unbuttoned his overcoat. Made for the bitter cold, it was much too heavy for indoors. "You not only disparage Everleigh, but you besmirch me with your innuendos, and I assure you, I don't take kindly to insults or to my honor being sullied."

What a malicious harpy. It was a wonder Chatterton, the younger, didn't do himself in, married to a shrew-like her.

Except for the minutest flinch, Everleigh maintained her poise.

"On second thought, Your Grace, I should like a witness to my conversation with Caroline. A man of standing whose word is respected and who can vouch for what is said."

Irritation crimped Caroline's mouth. "That's really not necessary—"

"Oh, but it is. If you want me to stay and listen to this *proposition*." Everleigh folded her arms. "You see, I've learned to protect myself, and I have you and the other Chattertons to thank for making me so cautious."

Caroline's fuming gaze waffled between Griffin and Everleigh. Lips pursed and looking like she'd sucked moldy bread, she gave a condescending sigh. "I truly don't understand why you must always be so difficult."

"I'm hungry and cold, Caroline. Get on with it before I change my mind."

Everleigh removed her bonnet as she spoke.

"Oh, very well." Caroline leveled Griffin a peeved glare, but he merely cocked a brow in response.

"I believe I can help you with the unpleasant tattle I've heard of late. I shall squash any murmurings I hear about your involvement in Arnold's and Frederick's deaths in exchange for ten thousand pounds." Caroline declared it as if granting a royal pardon.

Griffin barely stifled an incredulous snort. She had nerve; he'd give her that. Not a jot of common decency, however.

Her gaze skittered away from his reproachful stare.

A hint of color highlighting her cheekbones, she

tilted her pointed chin to a haughty angle. "I also promise not to ask for any more funds."

How magnanimous.

"Let me make sure I understand you clearly." Everleigh waggled her bonnet toward the other woman. "If I concede to your blackmail—for that's what this is—you'll squelch the rumors *you* started? Do you think me an imbecile? You'll squander any monies I give you just as you did those I already paid you, and then you'll demand more."

Everleigh was absolutely right. Mrs. Chatterton was a parasite who'd keep coming back as long as she believed her extortion would work.

"I wouldn't be too anxious to turn down my offer. I can destroy you." Caroline advanced toward Everleigh, all semblance of civility having flown. "You'd best be careful an accident doesn't befall you as well."

"Have you forgotten I'm standing here, Mrs. Chatterton?" Griffin said, squaring his shoulders. "For that sounded very much like a threat to me. You'd best hope nothing does happen to Everleigh because yours is the first name I'll give the authorities, along with a sworn statement that I heard you threaten her."

Stepping forward, he blocked her path to Everleigh. "I think you should leave now."

"I'm leaving, but rest assured, Everleigh, you haven't seen or heard the last from me." Caroline jerked on one of her gloves as she stomped away.

"By the by, Caroline. . .?" Everleigh pulled at the tips of one gloved hand.

Caroline glared over her shoulder as she crammed her hand into the other unfortunate glove.

"If anything *should* happen to me, Rayne and my cousins have been named my heirs." Everleigh had unclasped her cloak and, after shrugging it from her shoulders, lay it across an arm. Tone as frosty as the ground outside, she said, "You won't get a six-pence, even in a Christmas pudding. However, if you are willing to sign a contract with very specific terms, I may consider advancing you funds one *final* time."

Caroline let loose an oath Griffin had only heard seasoned doxies use before as she flounced down the corridor.

"I do believe that was a no."

His jest earned him a slight smile as they made their way toward the stairs.

"Everleigh, you don't owe her anything."

"I know, but I also know how utterly terrifying it is to be a woman without anything in a man's world. If she agrees in writing to never bother me again, it would be worth it. I'll consult with my solicitor after the first of the year and see what he suggests."

Something pleasant tumbled against his ribs.

"Does that mean you're staying for the duration of the house party then?"

Why did her answer matter so much?

He was wasting time with her: a woman who might be a splendid mother to Sarah but had no interest in marrying. What he ought to be doing was determining if any of the other female guests would make a suitable mother. And if he found one that would, could he abide being married to her, let alone faithful, for the decades to come?

That shouldn't be too terribly hard to tolerate since he still intended to travel extensively—at least six months out of the year. He'd already postponed a trip to Greece and another to Rome since bringing Sarah to England.

Could he bear being away from Sarah that long? He'd grown quite attached to the little minx and she to him.

Everleigh remained silent as they ascended the first flight of stairs. One of her hairpins had come loose and was in danger of slipping from her hair.

Griffin drew her to a halt before the stairway to their floor.

She cast him a questioning look.

"Just a moment. Your hairpin is coming out."

He pushed the pearl-capped pin into her hair, taking a moment to brush a finger across the soft strands. Her hair really was extraordinary, as fair as milk. No wonder Sarah had asked if she was an angel.

Everleigh's perfume—light, faintly tinted with vanilla and perhaps lilies—wafted upward, the scent as addictive as any opioid.

Neck bent, she remained absolutely motionless.

A gut-wrenching thought pummeled him.

Was she afraid of him?

Or did she grieve for her daughter?

Insensitive clod. He'd nearly forgotten the significance of the day.

"Everleigh?"

Very slowly and just as gently, he placed a bent finger beneath her chin and edged it upward.

"Are you afraid of me?"

Her brilliant green eyes rounded before her gold-tipped lashes fluttered downward, fanning her high cheekbones. Color blossomed beneath the dark fringe. No Ice-Queen here. In fact, other than that brief interlude when she said she was going to leave, she'd been almost cordial to him.

Griffin brushed his thumb across her chin, just below her peach-tinted lower lip. Each time he touched her skin, the satiny smoothness awed him.

"Are you?"

She shook her head. "No. At least I don't think I am, but you make me uneasy in a queer way."

His chest expanded in profound relief. Everleigh didn't even realize what she felt was carnal awareness.

Desire. No wonder, considering the abuse she'd suffered. He'd wager his favorite horse she didn't trust her instincts.

That was fine.

He trusted his, and the woman standing uncertainly before him was curious but timid. Had she ever been kissed with tenderness?

She still hadn't moved, nor had she opened her eyes.

Flattening a palm at the small of her back, he drew her ever nearer.

"Everleigh, I want to kiss you, but I shan't if it will make you afraid or if you don't want me to."

A lengthy moment passed and, just when he was about to suggest they continue to the nursery, she lifted her mouth.

Humility overwhelmed him that this gentle woman, who had no reason to trust him, would gift him not only with her trust, but a kiss from her luscious lips.

Slowly, so he wouldn't startle her, he lowered his head and barely brushed her lips with his.

She stiffened, then relaxed, a small smile playing around the edges of her mouth.

He kissed her again, this time pressing his mouth to hers a bit more firmly but making no attempt to deepen the kiss. She wasn't ready for that level of intimacy yet.

"See, that wasn't so awful, was it?"

Her eyelids slowly drifted upward, and wonder shone in her eyes before a mischievous gleam entered them, making the gold shards in her irises glint.

She swatted his arm.

"As if I'd tell you. You're already too full of yourself. I shall admit it wasn't too terribly dreadful."

He chuckled, absolutely enthralled with this playful, bantering Everleigh.

As they continued to the nursery, he couldn't keep from asking her again.

"Will you stay for all of the Duchess of Sutcliffe's festivities? Please."

By all that is holy, man.

He was all but pleading.

And toward what end?

If she let me kiss her, might she not also let me woo her?

A lot could happen in a December with a determined duke. Wasn't the season supposed to be one of miracles?

Head bent, mouth flattened into a considering line, she pondered his question.

He liked that about her. She thought before she spoke or reacted.

She gave him a small, almost shy smile.

"I shall stay."

6

Late that afternoon, the Duchess of Sutcliffe gathered her guests in the dining room.

At once Griffin sought out Everleigh.

She stood chatting with her cousins and Miss Twistleton.

That Twistleton chit was going to give some man a merry chase. Thank God it wouldn't be him, no matter how lovely she might be. The Breckensole misses weren't easily managed either.

He preferred Mrs. Chatterton's demure presence, especially since he now knew it hid a passionate woman with a spirited disposition and a generous heart.

"Sheffield, I should warn you, my wife has planned couples' charades after supper. I believe the theme is Christmastide traditions." Sutcliffe gave him a conspiratorial wink. "I know your feelings about the game. You might want to join some of the other chaps and I for billiards instead. We'll probably indulge in something a mite stronger than mulled cider."

Sutcliffe's brandy was legendary stuff.

He followed Griffin's focus to Everleigh nodding at something Miss Ophelia said.

"Or mayhap you'll want to participate in the antics after all. My understanding is the ladies also made several kissing boughs." Sutcliffe canted his dark head toward the dining room doorway where a gaily beribboned bundle of berry-laden holy and mistletoe hung suspended from a bright gold ribbon. "Thea fretted that one bough wasn't sufficient with this many guests. Especially if there would be enough berries to last till the end of the month."

Griffin furrowed his brow, not altogether keen on taking his turn with the pudding. Nonsensical traditions held little interest for him, but that was probably because his parents hadn't bothered with such trivialities. Truth to tell, they hadn't troubled themselves with their only child much either.

They'd died when he was at Eton, though he'd rarely gone home for the holiday anyway. That changed when Uncle Jerome assumed guardianship. However, Uncle, a confirmed bachelor—*until now*—hadn't a clue about Christmas falderal either. He'd introduced Griffin to the world by letting him travel with him.

Not a bad trade-off in his estimation.

"I don't take your meaning." Griffin glanced to the head of the table where Dandridge, looking like he'd been made to swallow mothballs, was taking his turn at stirring the fruity goop in the bowl.

Griffin made a mental note to keep his countenance expressionless when his turn came. "What do numerous blobs of berry-covered greenery have to do with me?"

"What he means, Sheffield, is you haven't taken your eyes off Everleigh Chatterton since you entered the room. More accurately, you haven't let her out of your sight since she entered the drawing room last night."

Pennington offered that observation with a hearty slap to Griffin's shoulder.

"I must say, I didn't think she was your type," Westfall said. "Far too starchy and frigid."

The thought of their earlier kiss heated Griffin's blood once more. She wasn't frosty at all. Merely abused and afraid.

"She's not cold, just cautious," he denied.

"*Brrrr*. My privates shrivel just walking past her." Smiling wickedly, Pennington gave a dramatic shiver and rubbed his arms.

Never before had Griffin had the urge to pop Pennington's cork, but, at the moment, wiping the cocky grin from his friend's handsome face held real appeal. Except, he was certain it would diminish his standing in Everleigh's opinion, and it mattered a great deal what she thought of him.

Eye to eye with Sutcliffe, Griffin folded his arms. "You presume I'd trap Mrs. Chatterton beneath a bough and demand a kiss?"

No need for entrapment.

She'd been willing.

Lord help him if they ever found out she'd already granted him that sweet favor. He'd never hear the end of it. The duke who managed to thaw the Ice-Queen. Sounded like a bad title to a gothic novel.

"She couldn't say no," Sutcliffe said with a furtive half-wink.

Just as a wife couldn't refuse her husband's attentions, curse Chatterton to purgatory.

"It's bad luck to refuse a kiss on the cheek, old chap," Westfall weighed in.

For pity's sake. Did he truly look so love-struck that his chums had to give him advice on how to woo a woman? Griffin wasn't exactly an inexperienced milksop or a monk who needed instruction.

"You're getting way ahead of yourselves." He wasn't allowing anyone else to speculate about him and Everleigh. "You do her a disservice as well, and that's beneath you."

To a man, they had the decency to look chagrined.

They truly were decent chaps at heart.

Voice lowered for Griffin's ears only, Sutcliffe said, "She deserves a bit of happiness. I don't know all the details, only the bits and buttons Theadosia has shared with me, but Mrs. Chatterton has had a very rough time."

Life was deuced unfair sometimes.

The duchess tapped a wooden spoon against the large bowl sitting at one end of the table. "Can I have everyone's attention, please?"

Griffin nearly shouted yes. Now his friends could leave off interfering in his romantic endeavors.

Gradually the excited chatter trickled to silence.

She fairly beamed, clearly enjoying herself.

"As you know, today is Stir-up Sunday. My father always quoted the *Common Book of Prayer* before stirring the pudding. As this is the first Christmas James, Jessica, and I shall celebrate the Yuletide without our parents, I hope you will indulge me as I give the blessing."

Almost defrocked after helping himself to tithes and other church funds, a disgraced Mr. Brentwood and his wife now shepherded a flock of soldiers and convicts in Australia.

The duchess closed her eyes and bowed her head.

Everyone else followed suit.

"Stir up, we beseech thee, O Lord, the wills of thy faithful people; that they, plenteously bringing forth the fruit of good works, may by thee be plenteously rewarded; through Jesus Christ our Lord. Amen."

"Amen," everyone murmured.

Holding the spoon like a magical wand, or perhaps a royal scepter, her grace waved it over the bowl.

"Cook has prepared and mixed the ingredients for our Christmas pudding, and we have the wooden spoon to represent Christ's rib. Everyone will have a chance to stir it. Make sure you stir in a clockwise direction thrice, and as you do, make three silent wishes. One is sure to come true. I'll go first to demonstrate."

She closed her eyes and stirred three times. When she opened her lids, her loving gaze met her husband's, and their adoration for each other was so obvious, Griffin felt slightly discomfited, as if he'd invaded a private moment between them.

He couldn't prevent a covert glimpse toward

Everleigh.

From beneath her lashes, she observed him as well but averted her gaze when she noticed his perusal. A rosy hue stained her cheeks as she followed the others to the table for her turn to stir dessert.

"It'll be the best-stirred pudding of all time after we're through," Pennington muttered drolly as he stepped into the queue.

"Indeed." Griffin chuckled. "And I believe the staff will have turns as well."

Pennington arched incredulous brows over his one blue eye and one green eye. "With the same pudding?"

Griffin jockeyed a shoulder. "I dunno."

"Rather than a fork or spoon, we'll need a teacup to sip it Christmas Day," Pennington said. "I suppose, then, my chance of finding the wishbone is next to none."

"As if you need any more luck, my friend. Besides, I suspect the duchess will have made sure the pudding is full of coins and other charms." Griffin wouldn't mind finding the ring. The finder was said to be certain to be married within a year.

"Yes, well, I'm not having any luck getting Gabriella Breckensole to spare me so much as a smile," Pennington muttered. "I declare she acts affronted each time I draw near, and I cannot imagine what I've done to offend."

Had Pennington at last found a woman who captured his serious interest?

Was that such a surprise?

Griffin had as well. His attention strayed to Everleigh once more.

Or maybe, if providence smiled upon him, he would find the ring. Mayhap he'd bribe the cook to add a score of rings to the pudding. He almost laughed out loud at the notion. By Jupiter, that could have all of the devilish dukes leg-shackled within a year.

He just might do it. Just to see the flummoxed expressions on their faces when they spooned their pudding.

Griffin shuffled forward a few paces, the enthusiasm of the others creating a jovial atmosphere. To his surprise, he actually contemplated what his three wishes ought to be.

Not surprisingly, one centered on the beauty who'd befuddled him since they first met.

Guest after guest dutifully stirred the pudding and made their wishes.

The men made quick work of it, laughing or jesting self-consciously while the women took the matter more seriously. Many closed their eyes, and a few of the ladies' mouths moved silently, almost prayerfully, as they made their wishes.

"Where's Sarah, Your Grace?"

Everleigh had made her way to his side and looked around as if she expected Sarah and Nurse to pop out from behind him or from beneath the table's lacy cloth.

"Didn't you bring her with you? Surely she must have her turn as well." Disappointment tinged her voice.

Over her fair head, Westfall waggled his eyebrows at Griffin.

Bloody ponce.

He couldn't tell Westfall to sod off or even give him a cease-your-idiocy glare without alerting

Everleigh. He'd not risk her realizing she was the subject of his friends' speculation, even if it weren't malicious.

Instead, he smiled and bent his neck to softly say, "She's a trifle young to understand the meaning, don't you think?"

"Oh, but that's why she needs her chance. Yuletide is a magical time for children. They are so innocent, their wishes so pure." She clasped his forearm. "If you hurry, you can bring her down in time. I'll await my turn until she's here."

How could he resist?

He sketched a half-bow. "I'll return momentarily."

Aware several other males' amused gazes followed him from the room, Griffin took care not to seem too eager. But the minute he was out of their eyesight, he hightailed it to the nursery, and perplexing poor Mrs. Schmidt, scooped Sarah into his arms.

"She needs to stir the pudding and make her wishes," he said, quite out of breath from sprinting up two flights of stairs.

Sarah giggled and clasped his neck as he dashed

back down the corridor from whence he'd come mere seconds before.

"I gets a wish, Papa?"

"Three wishes, cherub." He clomped down the first flight but slowed his pace to catch his breath on the second. He might have to plant one of his friends a facer if they laughed at him galloping back into the dining room.

He kissed the top of Sarah's head. "You'll stir the pudding three times, and you'll make a wish with each stir. Do you understand, pet?"

She nodded, that riot of curls Nurse tried—unsuccessfully—to tame bouncing about her shoulders.

He took a deep breath and, once assured his pulse had returned to a somewhat normal rate, sauntered into the dining room. With deliberate intent, he avoided the other dukes' eyes.

Everleigh separated herself from her friends, and, a radiant smile lighting her face, she glided to his side.

He'd barely made it back in time.

Only Jessica Brentwood and Crispin, Duke of Banbridge, hadn't yet stirred the pudding. From the perturbed expression on her pretty face, Miss Brentwood wasn't succumbing to Bainbridge's fabled charm.

"Did you already stir the pudding, Mrs. Chatterton?" Griffin asked.

She nodded. "Yes, I decided it would be easier to help with Sarah if I did. You go ahead and stir, and Sarah can go last."

"Evlee." At once, Sarah extended her arms, wiggling her fingers.

Without hesitation, Everleigh placed Sarah on her hip, smoothing the child's aster blue gown over her legs.

"Hello, darling." Giving Griffin another smile, she took her place behind him at the end of the short line. "Have you ever stirred the Christmas pudding before?"

Suddenly shy with all the adults looking at her, Sarah shook her head and tucked her cheek into Everleigh's shoulder.

"It's the greatest fun," Everleigh said.

"The pudding contains all sorts of delicious ingredients: currants, raisins, spices, eggs, brown sugar or molasses, and other tasty things all mixed together. After that, coins and other charms with special meanings are added for people to find in their servings. Everyone takes a turn stirring it, and then on Christmas Day, it's served sprinkled with powdered sugar. It's utterly scrumptious!"

When it was Sarah's turn, Griffin pulled a chair before the table for her to stand upon.

Everyone's attention was on the child, indulgent smiles on their faces. Probably each was recalling their own childhood holiday joy.

Everleigh had been right. Sarah should experience this tradition.

Sarah gripped the spoon in her two small hands. She squinched her eyelids shut tight, then popped them open again.

"I gets three wishes?"

Griffin nodded. "Yes."

Eyes screwed tightly closed once more, she stirred once. "I wish for a white puppy named Clarence with a green ribbon 'round his neck."

A few swiftly muffled titters followed her sweet

declaration.

His gaze met Everleigh's.

They'd forgotten to tell Sarah to make her wishes silently. Well, at least he knew what to get her for Christmas. He'd have to ask Sutcliffe if he knew of any litters of puppies in the area.

Sarah stirred the conglomeration again. "I wish my dolly had a new gown."

What about new hair and eyes and stuffing? Or just another doll?

No, Sarah saw Maya through the eyes of love, so she didn't notice the doll's many flaws. If she wanted to put a new dress on the ramshackle toy, Griffin would see that Maya had a new frock.

Her face scrunched in concentration, she stirred a final time.

"I wish Evlee was my mama."

Busy with Theadosia's seemingly never-ending Christmastide activities, the next twelve days passed quickly. Each morning, weather permitting, Everleigh walked with Sarah and Mrs. Schmidt, and more often than not, Griffin joined them.

He hadn't today, and he also hadn't been at breakfast.

Others had also begun taking a morning constitutional. No surprise, given the rich foods and lack of occasion to exercise. During summer house parties, guests might play croquet or shuttlecock, practice archery, or go riding or boating, but there weren't nearly as many opportunities to be outdoors and stretch one's legs in the wintertime.

Today, Ophelia, Gabriella, and Jessica, arms entwined, walked ahead of Everleigh.

Ice skating was planned for next week, but since she'd never learned how to skate, she'd already decided to stay behind and work on her Christmas gift for Sarah: a new rag doll. A replica of Maya, wearing a crimson and gold striped dress—an exact match to the dress Everleigh was sewing for Sarah.

She'd picked up the material and supplies she needed in Colchester during a shopping excursion Theadosia had planned four days ago. Those who hadn't brought gifts and wanted to exchange presents on Christmas Day had been given the opportunity to purchase a few trinkets.

There'd been much whispering and covert tucking of small packages into coats or reticles and brown paper packages tied with strings carried to the carriages by patient footmen, including Hampton. He still looked at her with more interest than he ought to, but he'd not been impertinent again.

Ridgebrook smelled wonderfully of pine and other

greeneries. Thea had tossed aside the custom of waiting until Christmas Eve to decorate the house. Garlands, wreaths, and ribbons bedecked the doorways, fireplaces, and mantels. She created a truly festive atmosphere, and, each passing day, Everleigh relaxed a bit more.

Nearly every room bore signs of the holiday, and tonight, again flouting custom, they were to decorate the grand Christmas tree. Smaller trees had already been erected in most of the common rooms, complete with miniature scenes around their bases. For days, in the afternoons and evenings, as one guest or another entertained them with music or songs or even read aloud, others had strung popcorn, cranberries, cherries, and currants or created paper chains for the tree.

Cook had been busy making sweetmeats to stuff in crocheted baskets, and she'd made dozens of pretty cakes and shaped biscuits to hang by ribbons from the tree.

Theadosia's propensity to toss aside custom to entertain her guests and provide them with a Christmastide they would long remember was endearing. She'd forgone no expense or effort to assure them an unforgettable holiday, especially Everleigh.

Everleigh hadn't told Griffin she planned on giving Sarah a gift for Christmas, fearing he'd feel obliged to reciprocate. It wouldn't be proper to accept anything from him, so she saved them both potential awkwardness by being secretive.

As it was, she was a touch discomfited he hadn't attempted to kiss her again.

She wasn't certain whether she was relieved or vexed. For the first time in her life, she'd enjoyed a man's touch, his warm lips upon hers, and, after that first kiss, she'd even briefly entertained the notion of taking a lover.

If he was the man sharing her bed, that was.

Young and healthy, she was curious to know what all the whispering and giggling was about, and even dear Theadosia had tried to explain that physical intimacy could be wonderful. After Frederick's assault and Arnold's clumsy molestations, until Everleigh had met Griffin—well, until he'd kissed her—she'd thought she could be perfectly content being celibate.

Then again, she'd never desired a man until she met him.

The more time she spent with Griffin, the stronger her yearnings grew, and she feared she'd make a cake of herself one of these days. The wisest course of action would be to leave, but she didn't want to go home now.

Plain and simple, she liked being with him. She enjoyed being with Sarah too.

In fact, Everleigh had even begun to appreciate the comradery of the dukes, though the ten scoundrels teased and harassed one another incessantly.

The storm that had threatened the other day had passed them by, but as she eyed the low-hanging, petulant clouds today, she felt certain their luck was about to change. There'd be snow by nightfall, or she wasn't blonde, and that wasn't a doe peering hesitantly from yonder tree-line.

When she could cuddle beneath a warm throw before the fire and read a novel while savoring a strong cup of tea, she enjoyed the snow. There'd been so much commotion at Ridgewood every day, finding a quiet niche to read in hadn't been possible.

The only respite she found from the constant tumult was in her bedchamber. A padded window seat ran the full length of the turreted window and provided an exceptional view of the countryside. Even so, she hadn't spent much time there, except to sew Sarah's presents.

Everleigh hadn't thought she was terribly lonely before, especially with Rayne's company, but there was something to be said for the gaiety of gatherings with friends.

She quirked her mouth at her musings.

Was this the same woman who dreaded assemblies just a few days ago?

It was the guests.

Thea had been true to her word. Except for Caroline that first day, the men and women were nothing like the sots and degenerates Arnold had regularly entertained.

Her eyes bright and face ruddy from the cold, Sarah skipped along the gravel path. Maya, appearing more bedraggled than ever, trailed along the ground as

Sarah hopped on one foot, then the other.

"Evlee?"

"Yes, darling?"

"Read to me before I sleeps t'night?"

Everleigh slid Mrs. Schmidt a glance.

Worry puckered the sweet woman's face. She also fretted that Sarah was growing too attached.

"I shall have to check with your Papa, but I think I might be able to. It also depends on what the Duchess of Sutcliffe has planned for this evening. Why don't you go inside now and have your hot chocolate?"

That had become a tradition as well.

Sarah bobbed a little curtsy and clasped Nurse's hand. "You come too?"

Everleigh shook her head and gathered her cloak a bit closer. "Not today. I have some things I need to attend to."

After the mortifying incident with the Christmas pudding, Everleigh had almost ordered the carriage brought 'round to take her home straightaway. She wouldn't have believed a room could grow so completely silent so speedily, but there wasn't a doubt everyone had heard the child's last wish.

Theadosia had hugged Sarah while claiming the spoon and redirected everyone's attention. "Let's all adjourn to the drawing room for a cup of mulled wine, shall we? I have another surprise for you."

That was when she announced the treasure hunt for tomorrow, and, also, since they'd missed exchanging gifts on December 6th, St. Nicholas's Day, those that wanted to do so, would now exchange gifts on Christmas Day.

"Mrs. Chatterton." Griffin waved at her from the pathway leading to the stables. "Might I have a word?"

He'd no sooner asked than snowflakes began drifting down.

"Snow!" Sarah squealed and stuck her tongue out, trying to catch the fat, fluffy flakes.

"Goodness, child," Mrs. Schmidt fussed. "Let's get you inside before you catch your death."

It wouldn't have hurt to allow Sarah a few moments in the snow, but Everleigh refused to interfere. Sarah was Mrs. Schmidt's charge, and, as Griffin had said, she wasn't a biddable child. Nurse had difficulty reining the child in without others throwing a wrench into her efforts.

The truth was, the cold probably aggravated Mrs. Schmidt's arthritic bones.

Should Everleigh suggest to Griffin a younger, more energetic woman, a governess perhaps, might be in order? It wasn't her place, of course, but Mrs. Schmidt wasn't quite up to snuff, and though she obviously held Sarah in great affection, she was also a bit lax in areas.

Perhaps later, when the house party neared its end, Everleigh might voice her thoughts. For now, she'd keep her own council.

She made her way to Griffin, wearing a shocking red, green, and yellow knitted scarf about his neck. It was quite the ugliest thing Everleigh had ever seen. She tried not to stare, but her gaze kept wandering back to the atrocity.

He chuckled, that wonderful resonance deep in his chest she'd grown to enjoy, much to her befuddlement, and pulled the ends tighter. "Widow Beezley insisted I accept it as thanks for purchasing a spaniel puppy from her."

Everleigh clapped her hands and practically bounced on her toes. "For Sarah?"

"Yes. I have her in the stables, and the good lads there have agreed to watch the imp until Christmas for me."

"Oh, oh, it's a a *she*?" Would Sarah be terribly disappointed?

"Yes. The males were spoken for, and when I saw this little darling . . ." He grasped her elbow to help her over an uneven spot on the pathway. "Well, you'll see why I had to have her for Sarah."

Inside the stables, Everleigh paused for a moment. Smells of hay, horse liniment, manure, and grains filled the warm building. Horses knickered softly every now and again, and a tortious-shell cat padded down the pathway toward them between the stalls. It gave a plaintive meow, and another cat answered from the loft above them.

"Claire is down there."

He pointed to a stall at the far end.

"Claire rather than Clarence? Very clever, I must

say."

For a man having a child's care thrust upon him, he'd taken to the task of fatherhood with an aptitude many men lacked. He even permitted Sarah to call him Papa, and she couldn't think of another man she knew who would've allowed that.

He grinned, a trifle self-consciously, and lifted a shoulder. "It's the best I could come up with."

"I like it, and I think Sarah will too."

He slid the bolt and pushed the door open. In the corner, sitting on a blanket, was a tiny forlorn, black and tan King Charles Spaniel pup with curly ears. She stood and wagged her tail before toddling over to them.

"Oh, stars above, she's absolutely precious." Everleigh sank to her knees, and the puppy clambered into her lap. "I always wanted a puppy as a little girl, but Mama said we couldn't afford one."

Maybe she should get a dog.

She'd enjoy the company, especially when Rayne married.

Griffin knelt on one knee beside her and ran his

hand down Claire's back. "With those ears, she reminded me of Sarah."

Everleigh giggled as Claire nibbled her nose and licked her cheeks.

"She's absolutely perfect. Well done, you. Sarah will be ecstatic." She kissed the pup's head. "Don't forget the green ribbon."

Rubbing her face into the puppy's soft fur, she gave him a sideways look.

He touched her cheek then leaned over and skimmed his mouth across hers.

Heaven.

Instinct prompted her to open her lips, and he slid his tongue into her mouth. Not invasive or violating, but in tenderness and gentle exploration.

Nothing else mattered: not the puppy in her arms, the fresh straw she knelt upon, the swirling snow outside, or that she was afraid of men and had vowed never to be vulnerable again.

She simply savored the experience and Griffin. His taste. His essence of soap and starch and something faintly spicy. His hard-muscled thighs pressing into hers, and his lips at once firm but soft, teaching her how to kiss.

After several blissful moments, Claire must've decided she didn't like being ignored, for she nipped his chin.

"Ouch." He lifted his mouth from Everleigh's. "She's punctured me, I do believe."

Everleigh *tisked* as she held the little darling to her neck. "I think you'll live."

"Everleigh."

Griffin cupped the back of her neck, his gaze so penetrating her heart slowed.

"What is it?"

"Marry me. I have no doubt you'd make Sarah a wonderful mother, and I've never encountered a woman as extraordinary as you."

Marry him? Marry him?

Was he queer in the attic?

Barely over a week ago, she'd sworn never to wed again. She had far too much to lose by doing so, not the least of which was her independence. Griffin would assume all control of her wealth. All control of every aspect of her life, even her body.

She opened her mouth to tell him just that, but he held up his hand.

"Please hear me out. Please."

Reluctant, battling renewed apprehension, she gave a shallow nod.

"Thank you." He pressed his mouth to her knuckles.

"I know we've only known each other for a short time, but there's a connection between us. You sense it too. I know you do. I realize you aren't ready yet. But I want you to know that I feel something for you. I don't understand exactly what it is, but I also don't want to dismiss it as nothing. It is something powerful and rare. Don't answer now. Just think about it. Can you do that much?"

Gaze lowered, she ran her fingers through Claire's fur.

What could it hurt?

Everleigh wasn't making a commitment or promising to accept his addresses. She didn't even agree to let him court her. The silence grew lengthy. At last she raised her head.

"I shall consider it, under one condition, and you have to promise to accept my decision afterward."

He ran a finger along her jawbone. "All right. What is your condition?"

"You will come to my bedchamber tonight and make love to me. I know it's immoral and a sin." Heat scorched her cheeks but she plowed onward. "And I honestly don't know if I shall be able to go through with the act. Nonetheless, I must know if it's even possible for me to enjoy sexual congress before I would ever consider exchanging vows again."

"Everleigh…"

She held up a staying finger. "If people who have never experienced the abuse that I have believe they have the right to judge me for…" Lord, she could scarcely say the word. "Fornicating, then they can take their self-righteousness up with the Lord."

She rolled a shoulder as she brushed a fingertip across an eyebrow. Both actions lessened the tension that made Everleigh feel as if she'd snap like a dry twig if she as much as sneezed.

"If I cannot, we both know it would be foolish to pursue a relationship. You wouldn't want a wife who couldn't bear your touch. If I don't find the act as horrific as my singular experience was, then perhaps we can contemplate what a future together might look like."

An uncomfortable minute passed as his dark gaze searched her face. He ran his thumb and forefinger down the bridge of his nose.

"I confess, I'm conflicted, Everleigh. I feel it would be dishonorable to bed you outside the bonds of marriage. You might get with child."

She might. She had before.

A grin kicked his mouth up on one side. "Though don't think for an instant that I don't find you irresistible."

Turning her mouth downward, she scrunched her forehead. "I . . ." Gads, but this was awkward. "I thought there were ways to prevent conception."

"There are, but you wouldn't have a complete experience." He set the puppy aside. "Do you understand what that means?"

Good Lord. Here they were kneeling in a horse stall, chatting about *sex* when at any moment a stable hand might come upon them. She might be known as the Ice-Queen, but she'd not have her reputation in tatters.

"I believe I do, and I also believe it is time to return to the house."

She stood and cautiously looked around.

Thank goodness. They were still alone.

Griffin stood as well.

"What time should I come to your chamber?"

8

Everleigh paced back and forth, and each time she passed the fireplace, she glanced at the bronze and ormolu clock atop the carved cherry wood mantel.

Half-past eleven. And Griffin still hadn't arrived.

A cozy fire snapped and crackled cheerily in the hearth, and candles flickered on the bedside tables and in the wall sconces in readiness for their assignation.

She'd told him to come at eleven o'clock. She pleaded a headache and retired by nine to have a leisurely bath and bring her rioting nerves under control.

Now, pacing to and fro in her chamber, snow billowing from the sky as it had for the past twelve hours, she bit her lower lip.

Had she misread him?

Miscalculated?

Been too forward?

He'd said he desired her and had agreed to come to her chamber, so where was he?

A deep sigh escaped her, and after a final glance at the clock, she wandered to the window seat. A pristine, virginal blanket of snow at least a foot deep covered the grounds. At dinner, there'd been talk of sleigh rides tomorrow.

Drawing her knees to her chest, she rested her cheek on them.

What had she been thinking, making such an immoral suggestion? She'd already asked God to forgive her multiple times. She'd probably shocked Griffin so badly he'd decided he didn't want a woman of her immoral ilk for his wife after all. What man would want someone with *that* character flaw around a child?

A tear crept down her cheek.

Goose.

She wiped it away with the back of her hand.

How she would face him tomorrow, she couldn't imagine. What was more, in this snow, going home was dangerous. Likely impossible. She'd just have to hold her chin up and pretend she hadn't been a brazen nincompoop.

After a final glance outside, she padded barefoot across the room and extinguished the candles in the sconces. She blew out the tapers on one of the nightstands then removed her robe.

Shivering despite the fire, she fluffed a pillow.

The knock was so faint, she wasn't sure she'd heard it.

She paused, head cocked toward the door.

There it was again, the merest scraping.

She flew across the room, her hair billowing around her shoulders. Holding her breath, she cracked the door open.

Hair damp and attired in only a shirt and pantaloons, Griffin stood there.

"Quickly, open up. I should hate to have to explain to Mrs. Schmidt what I'm doing fresh from my bath outside your chamber."

Everleigh swung the door wide, and once he'd entered, glanced up and down the passageway, then closed it and turned the key in the lock.

"I didn't think you were coming."

"The chaps decided to ruminate about old times over multiple bottles of Sutcliffe's brandy. It was no small feat nursing my single glass without them catching on. I finally escaped, using a need to look in on Sarah as an excuse."

He gave her a sly wink. "I'm finding having a child has more advantages than I realized."

Now nerves overwhelmed Everleigh. She didn't know what to say or do.

Her uncertainty must've shown.

"Come here, darling."

Griffin opened his arms wide, and she rushed into his embrace.

He alone made her feel safe.

"We don't have to do this. I'd much rather my ring was on your finger before we do." He kissed the top of her head.

She wasn't sure she could ever let any man put a ring on her hand again.

"I need this, Griffin."

She wrapped her arms around his solid waist and clung to him, trying to make him understand why it was so important.

"Frederick Chatterton despoiled me, and Arnold could never complete the act. Trust me, he tried many, *many* times and took out his frustration with his fists and, at times, a cane. I've never known a man's gentle touch, never experienced passion. I don't know if I can."

She tilted her head back and noticed his smooth-shaven jaw. He'd taken the time to shave too.

"But I think if I am capable, it must be with you. For you do something to me, Griffin."

His eyes had gone flinty, and his face granite hard.

"If those two sods weren't already dead, I'd kill them," he said.

"Let's not let them ruin this. I only mentioned them to help you understand why I am the way I am. I trust you, but if I cannot do this, if I displease you somehow, I have to believe I am flawed. That I really am frigid, and I was never meant to know physical gratification."

He cupped her face, his expression so tender that tears welled in her eyes.

"You are not flawed, Everleigh. And you are most certainly not frigid. I am humbled at the trust you've put in me."

He lifted her into his arms and carried her to the turned-down bed.

~*~

Much later, Griffin pulled Everleigh into his embrace, her luminous head resting in the crook of his shoulder. He traced little circles on her lower back.

"Does this mean you'll marry me?" he asked.

He'd fallen in love with her.

Probably had that moment in the drawing room when she'd lifted a frightened Sarah into her arms.

Everleigh stiffened, then sighed as she rolled onto her back and slung an elbow over her eyes.

"I said I'd think about it, Griffin."

Disappointment, sharp and jagged, pierced him in the gut. He'd been so sure he'd broken through Everleigh's defenses. That she'd agree to wed him now. It seemed there was more than just fear of intimacy he needed to overcome.

"One step at a time then, sweet." He caressed her shoulder. "What else are you afraid of?"

She lifted her head, her eyes more emerald than jade in the muted light. The thick cloud of her moon spun hair brushed his chest.

"How do you know there is something else?" Her fair brows pulled together the tiniest bit.

She might be able to put on a bland façade other people couldn't see through, but this remarkable woman's eyes revealed much.

"I can see it in your eyes, darling."

Even now, the shutters that slammed shut when anyone—any man—ventured too close fell into place.

She stared at his chin and spoke softly, haltingly.

"I fear . . . losing my independence. I shan't ever subject myself to a man's whims again. *Ever.* If I marry, my husband has complete control over me. My wealth becomes his. My body becomes his to do with what he will. My children, if there are any, are also his to do with what he wants. As a woman, I have no rights. None."

What she said was true.

A woman was at her husband's mercy.

Everleigh sank onto the pillow, her back against him and whispered, "That's what I'm afraid of, Griffin. I cannot endure that life again. I cannot."

She curled into a ball, weeping softly.

He pulled her into his arms, needing to comfort her.

"I would sign a settlement allowing you to retain all of your wealth, Everleigh. I vow I would never lay a hand on you in anger. As for children, I think they need their mother, which is why I want to find a woman who can love Sarah as her own. I believe you are that woman."

"You have more faith in me than I have in myself."

After tenderly kissing her neck, he rose.

"I'd love to stay with you, but I shan't risk your reputation. Nor shall I rush you. Wounds such as yours take time to heal."

He came around to the other side of the bed and knelt there.

She opened her eyes, the lashes dark and spiky from her tears.

He palmed her damp cheek.

"I've fallen in love with you, Everleigh Chatterton. I shall wait as long as it takes, do whatever I need to do to convince you of that. I'll help you overcome your qualms. My love will heal your fears."

She swallowed, then licked her lower lip.

"You are a good man, Griffin, kind and decent and generous, but I cannot make any promises. It wouldn't be fair to either of us. I need to take things one day at a time. I don't have your confidence. I'm afraid to trust my feelings for you."

"I know." He tucked the bedclothes around her shoulders in much the same manner as he did Sarah. "But *I* trust your feelings, and I have confidence enough for the both of us."

"Humble blighter, aren't you?" She attempted a wobbly smile.

"Go for a sleigh ride with me tomorrow?" Brushing the hair from her face, Griffin paused and ran his fingers through the length before fanning the strands across the pillow. "Sarah's never been."

"Unfair." She hit him with a pillow. "How am I supposed to deny her that fun?"

She didn't look quite so tormented.

He wiggled his eyebrows.

"Madam, when I set out to win a woman's heart and hand, you have no idea what I'm capable of. Erect your ramparts and battlements if you must, but I believe my love will tear them down."

9

The next afternoon, bundled to their noses beneath furs and quilts, three sleighs full of the braver guests pulled into the courtyard that fronted Ridgewood. Jingling bells, the whoosh of the sleighs' rudders, and laughter filled the air.

Under cover of the blankets, Griffin held Everleigh's hand as he had most of the outing.

"Everleigh, the cold weather and these excursions agree with you. Why, you're positively incandescent," Miss Twistleton said, her face radiant.

Everleigh only smiled, but Griffin caught the furtive glance she sent him.

Hers was the complexion of a woman who'd been

fully satiated and still bore the afterglow.

Miss Twistleton's shiny countenance might be because Westfall had managed to seat himself beside her, the sly devil. Pennington, on the other hand, brooded like a woebegone mongrel. Miss Gabriella had taken one look at the sleigh he was in and marched to another, her nose pointed skyward.

Pennington had best turn his attention elsewhere, for that door had slammed shut and was bolted from within.

Sarah, sound asleep and mouth parted, curled against Everleigh's other side, Maya clutched in her mittened hand.

When they reached the mansion, Griffin climbed out first and reached for Sarah.

Everleigh laid her in his arms.

It had been on the tip of his tongue all day to ask if she'd thought any more about his marriage offer, but less than twenty-four hours had passed. He wouldn't rush her. If need be, he'd continue to court her after the house party ended, for he was adamant Everleigh Chatterton would be his duchess.

Everyone bustled into the foyer where much stamping of feet to remove snow earned them a starchy stare from Grover, standing beside three footmen ready to accept the myriad of coats, scarfs, capes, gloves, muffs, and hats from the chilled adventurers.

He raised his patrician nose an inch and announced, "There is an assortment of hot beverages and dainties for your enjoyment in the drawing room. Her Grace begs you to forgive her absence. She's feeling a trifle puny. She'll be present for dinner, however."

"I'll only be a few minutes." Griffin angled toward the stairs.

"I shall walk up with you," Everleigh said. "I'd rather take off my outer garments in my chamber. I need to straighten my hair in any event."

He thought she looked delightful, slightly mussed and windblown.

Falling into step beside him, she glanced behind her as she removed her gloves. "The poor footmen and Grover are taxed to their limits with this many people."

Griffin shifted Sarah so her head rested on his

shoulder.

"True, but they also receive vails from everyone, and with a house party this size, that means a substantial bonus for each of the servants before the holidays."

They parted on the landing. He continued to the nursery and Everleigh to her chamber.

"Griffin?"

"Yes?"

One hand cradling Sarah's head, he turned back toward Everleigh. She'd paused a couple of paces away.

She bit her lower lip and fidgeted with her gloves.

Were her cheeks still rosy from cold, or was she blushing?

He drew nearer and spoke low. "What is it?"

"I . . ."

Staring at the buttons on his coat, she flicked her tongue out to wet her lower lip.

Her attention shifted to Sarah, limp as her ragdoll in his embrace.

"Never mind. It's not important."

Whatever she wanted to say, she was afraid Sarah might overhear, even though the child hadn't so much as stirred for the last half an hour.

"Let me settle her in the nursery, and then we can talk. Do you want me to come to your chamber?"

Risky business that. But if Everleigh wanted privacy, her room or his was the best place to have a conversation.

Everleigh gave a short nod. "That's fine."

Twenty minutes later, he rapped on her door. Sarah had awakened and fussed for a few minutes when he laid her down, and after she'd drifted to sleep once more, he'd taken the time to go to his bedchamber and remove his greatcoat.

When Everleigh didn't answer, he knocked again.

Still no response.

He tried the handle, and the door clicked open. Poking his head inside, he looked around.

"Everleigh?"

Curled up on the window seat, one hand tucked beneath her cheek, she was fast asleep, minus her cloak and redingote. Those she'd tossed on her bed.

Common sense demanded Griffin leave and let her have her nap.

Bugger that.

Common sense wouldn't win this woman's heart.

After checking the corridor, he closed the door. He sat beside Everleigh and swept a curl off her forehead. She appeared so peaceful in slumber. He could watch her for hours.

What if his seed *had* found fertile soil in her womb?

Shutting his eyes, he pulled in a deep breath, both exhilarated and appalled at the prospect. Her first pregnancy revealed she was easily impregnated. He was an churl for agreeing to her request.

There was nothing for it. Everleigh might be carrying his child. He must convince her to marry him, and sooner rather than later.

She stirred, and her lashes fluttered open. Her drowsy smile held something more than sleep.

"I'm sorry. I must've dozed off."

She scooted into a sitting position, resting her back against the window casements before patting her mussed hair. Several tendrils had escaped their pins and curled over her shoulders.

He glanced out the window. It had begun to snow again. They'd returned from sleighing just in time. If the weather pattern held, the Sutcliffes might have guests longer than anticipated.

"I shouldn't have come in," Griffin said. "You're obviously tired."

"Yes, I didn't get a full night's sleep last night," she quipped with a saucy smile and a coy glance.

Now his Ice-Queen was flirting?

What next?

Perhaps she'd also laid awake the rest of last night.

"Indeed." The minx. He hadn't come here to make love to her again, no matter how enticing the idea might be. "But was it worth losing a little slumber over?"

"Oh, very, *very* worth it," she said.

She drew his head to hers and kissed him. "I've wanted to do that all day."

"I'm only too happy to oblige, sweetheart."

He waggled his eyebrows, and she giggled. He'd not deny himself her kisses.

Taking his hand between hers, she linked her slender fingers with his. "Will you come to me again tonight?"

So that was what she'd wanted to ask.

Her appetite had been whetted, and she was eager to practice more. No keener than Griffin was to teach her, but not by skulking about in darkened corridors and whispering clandestinely behind locked doors. No, when next she graced his bed, it would be as his wife.

He rubbed his thumb over the back of her hand.

She wasn't going to like what he had to say.

"Everleigh, last night was the most wonderful thing I've ever experienced." He squeezed her fingers. "But because I love you and won't risk impregnating you unless we're married, I must, with the deepest regret, refuse."

Her beautiful eyes rounded, and she pulled her hand away.

"Why must we marry? People take lovers all the time. Married people take lovers." She poked his chest, then made a curt gesture with her hand. "Lord knows I witnessed enough fornicating and adultery while married to Arnold."

Undoubtedly witnessed things no respectable woman could ever admit.

Her frustrated gaze impaled him. "You've had lovers. Probably dozens of them, and don't tell me you haven't."

"Not dozens, darling, but I am flattered you think me so irresistible."

She punched him in the shoulder. Hard.

"Arrogant, conceited jackanape."

Checking the grin that tickled his lips, Griffin rubbed his arm where she'd struck him. By Jove, beneath that cool exterior, her blood and spirit ran hot. This Everleigh would keep him on his toes. What a delightful prospect.

Green sparks flew from her irises, and her anger gave him hope.

She was jealous.

"Maybe I'll take a lover too."

She flung her head back, giving vent to her

frustration.

"I'm sure I can find a man to accommodate me."

Over my dead body.

In a way, he was flattered she'd so enjoyed their encounter that she had braved approaching him.

He forced calmness into his tone. "I cannot deny I've been with other women, nor will I apologize for what's gone on before you. However, I shall never knowingly put you in the situation that forced you to marry Chatterton."

"Since when did you get so blasted noble?" she snapped.

He cupped her shoulders and gave her the gentlest shake, forcing her to look at him.

"I'll hear no more talk of you taking a lover. You could end up with someone who would abuse you. What we enjoyed is not typical." No, it had been beyond extraordinary.

"I have only your word on that." Lips pursed, she tormented the tassels of the pillow beside her. "How do I know you're not lying just to keep me to yourself?"

Not ready to concede defeat just yet, was she?

"I'm not, and I believe, deep inside, beyond your disappointment and frustration, you know that. Last night was something unbelievably special, and it should be treasured. Even now my child might be growing inside you."

Expression stricken, her mouth parted, and her gaze dived to her belly. She instinctively cradled her womb. Shoulders slumping, she shook her head.

"I thought . . ." She gazed out the window. "It doesn't matter."

Confound it. Griffin hated seeing Everleigh despondent.

"Everleigh, I'll give you all the time you need to grow to trust me. Unless you are with child. Then we would need to wed at once."

Fingering the locket at her throat, she thrust her chin upward.

"I've been down *that* road once already, and I'll be cursed—*cursed, I say*—if I'll do it again."

He could almost hear the ramparts *chinking* higher and higher as she erected self-protective fortifications around herself.

"If I ever marry again, it will be because I *want* to. Not because I *have* to." She pointed a shaky finger toward the door. "You should leave now. Last night was a stupid, stupid mistake. I apologize for imposing upon you."

"Everleigh . . ."

She presented her profile, her Ice-Queen facade firmly in place once more.

"Please don't approach me again. I'm leaving just as soon as the weather permits."

10

Christmas Day. At last.

The past two days had dragged on and on since Everleigh had told Griffin to leave her alone. She hadn't gone down to dinner that night but instead had cried herself to sleep, something she hadn't done since marrying Arnold.

Her frosty guise once more in place, she kept to the fringes of the activities.

Sarah's two gifts tucked beneath her arm, Everleigh held her emerald empire gown up with her other hand. What had possessed her to accept an early birthday present from Theadosia?

Surely it was the least she could do to thank her

dear friend, she told herself.

Maybe she'd wanted to impress Griffin as well?

Why, when she'd made clear her wishes?

She caught sight of herself in one of the corridor mirrors. The gown was truly lovely and befitting the season. It had been a long while since she'd worn anything so colorful, and despite her fragile heart, the gown lifted her spirits a notch.

Evening cloaked the subdued light visible through the windows. And beyond that, snow covered the picturesque landscape. A perfect setting for the holiday.

Griffin must've conspired with Fate to keep her at Ridgewood.

It had snowed intermittently since the sleigh ride, and a good two feet or more of white covered everything. It had been decades since anyone had seen a December with such deep snowfall in Essex. Leaving was nearly impossible, and even though she longed to flee to Fittledale Park, she wouldn't jeopardize a driver's safety for her own selfish wishes.

She'd endured marriage to Arnold for two years;

she could certainly abide a few more days here. The company was pleasant, the food exceptional, and Theadosia made sure no one was bored or overlooked. Still, even in a house this large, with the guests confined indoors, she couldn't help but encounter Griffin unless she stayed in her chamber.

Seeing him across the room hurt like a mule kick to her innards each time, but he'd respected her wishes and hadn't approached her. His gaze never left her though, and the hurt and frustration in his eyes caused hers to get misty more than once.

He was a good man, and he did love her.

She didn't doubt it.

Lying awake at night, reliving the passion they'd shared, recalling his witty rejoinders and the tenderness he showed her and Sarah, she'd come upon a startling discovery.

She might very well love him too.

No. Everleigh *did* love Griffin.

Fear had crippled her, warped her emotions, until she didn't even recognize what was before her. Shame infused her as she made her way to the drawing room where the great decorated pine tree stood. She'd used Griffin in the basest, meanest manner. Had their situations been reversed, she'd have thought him a monster for asking to bed her.

Her slippers whooshed on the marble floor as they had that first night. It seemed much longer than just over a fortnight ago.

What if she did carry his child?

An unwed woman ought to be dismayed at the thought, but she wasn't. She'd welcome a child—his child—no matter what.

She paused at the entry to the drawing room. As expected, guests milled about the room, and extra chairs were placed throughout. Candles winked on the grand tree, beneath which were stacked mounds of presents.

"Everleigh! Your gown is stunning." Gabriella grabbed her sister's arm. "Look at Everleigh, Fee-Fee. She's finally out of mourning."

That caused several heads to turn in her direction, one of which loomed above all the others.

Ophelia sent a not-so-covert peek toward Griffin.

Everyone probably thought the same thing she did, that Everleigh had set her cap for him.

Appreciation quirked his mouth the merest bit as his hot gaze trailed over her, and from across the room, she could almost hear him begging her to give them a chance.

"Evlee. Evlee." Bum upward, Sarah scrambled down from the settee. She ran to Everleigh and held out her arms. "Up."

Everleigh passed her gifts to Jessica. "Could you please give these to Mrs. Schmidt for me? They are for Sarah."

The gifts for her cousins and the others had been brought down earlier in the day, but she'd needed to put the finishing touches on Sarah's frock and doll.

"Of course." Jessica smiled, catching the nurse's eye. "You look lovely. Green is definitely your color. It matches your eyes."

Everleigh lifted Sarah. "Hello, darling. Happy Christmas."

"Happy Chris'mas, Evlee. I has a puppy. She has sharp teeth." Sarah twisted, and looking over

Everleigh's shoulder, inspected the floor. Her little face crumpled. "I think Papa sent Claire to the nurs'ry."

"I met your puppy. She's adorable, just like you." Everleigh hugged Sarah to her.

She'd miss the little mite.

She felt Griffin's gaze caressing her again as he murmured something to Hampton while accepting a glass of champaign.

Mrs. Schmidt accepted the packages and extended her hand. "Let's go for a walk and check on your puppy, shall we, love?"

A delicate way of saying it was time for Sarah to go to the nursery.

"Papa said I stay up late." Sarah's face contorted into a pout.

"You will, pet. You have more gifts to open." She held them up. "And after supper, you'll have plum pudding!" Mrs. Schmidt said. "Besides, this is Claire's first night in the house. She'll be afraid and lonely, and your puppy will want to cuddle with you."

Everleigh passed Sarah to her Nurse. "I'll come to

say goodnight to you too. I'd love to see your puppy again."

Sarah stuck her lower lip out. "Promise?"

"I promise."

She should've taken the gifts directly to the nursery, and had she been speaking to Griffin, she'd have known what his plans were for Sarah tonight.

She forced a smile as Nicolette approached.

"Everleigh, did you and Sheffield have a falling out?" Nicolette spoke low, but her eyes brimmed with worry.

Everleigh shrugged.

"Not exactly. It just wasn't meant to be."

"Bosh. What utter twaddle." Nicolette slanted her gaze toward him. "He cannot stop staring at you, and you're no better."

"Please leave it alone, Nicolette."

Everleigh didn't mean to sound cross, but neither could she discuss something so painful.

A fleeting look of surprise skated across Nicolette's face before she nodded. "All right. Come sit with me."

She grasped Everleigh's hand and towed her to chairs near the tree.

"I thought we were opening presents after supper?" Everleigh sank onto the gold and cream striped cushion.

"We are, but Theadosia said she wanted to make an announcement."

Just then, Theadosia, wearing a spectacular ice blue gown, floated into the drawing room on Sutcliffe's arm. She positively glowed tonight. As difficult as the past couple of days had been, she still deserved Everleigh's thanks for forcing her out of self-imposed isolation.

She had enjoyed herself—mostly.

Her attention gravitated to Griffin, only he wasn't there anymore. Swallowing, she lowered her gaze to her clasped hands.

She didn't blame him for leaving. She found it hard to be in the same room with him too.

How she wanted to take those words back. Tell Griffin to not stop trying to win her heart.

Why don't you?

Why indeed? She had nothing to lose.

Lifting her head, she searched the room. Drat and blast. He was truly gone, and she couldn't very well go in search of him. Not without raising brows. There was also the worry that he might not accept her apology.

She'd never know unless she tried. Her stomach wobbled with excitement.

Oh, and she had to try. She had to, for he was her everything. Nothing mattered but him, not her fears or concerns. Just Griffin and what they had together.

She started to rise when Theadosia clapped her hands. "Please have a seat or find a place you are comfortable standing for a few moments."

Sinking back onto the chair, Everleigh suppressed a frustrated sigh.

"We have an announcement to make." Sutcliffe stepped near and wrapped an arm around his wife's waist.

"Oh, what do you suppose it is?" Nicolette whispered in Everleigh's ear.

"Given the specialness of this day when we celebrate our Savior's birth, we thought it only fitting to tell our dearest friends and neighbors our good news." Theadosia gazed at Sutcliffe with utter adoration.

He lifted her hand and kissed her fingertips. "We are to be parents, come summer."

A chorus of congratulations echoed about the room, not the least of which was the Dowager Duchess's cry of delight.

Everleigh took advantage of the melee to slip from the room. She headed toward the stairs, thinking Griffin might've gone above to say good night to Sarah.

A movement in the dining room caught her eye.

Griffin?

What the deuce was he up to?

Looking very much like a naughty boy, he had moved the name tags around the table. From just outside the door, an amused smile curving her mouth, she watched him make a complete muddle of Theadosia's seating arrangements.

"I do hope, Griffin, this means you've placed yourself beside me."

He whirled around, one name card grasped between his fingers before a slow smile tinged with mischief arched his lips.

"I was just about to do so."

He set the card down then stood back to admire his handiwork.

"I've been doing a bit of matchmaking." He pointed. "Jessica Brentwood and Bainbridge. Miss Twistleton and Westfall. Miss Breckensole and Pennington—"

"You didn't!" Everleigh rushed forward a few steps. He had indeed. "You wicked, wicked man. Gabriella will never forgive you."

He strode to her and clasped her hand.

"It's not her forgiveness I crave. Everleigh, I rushed you. I tried to force something you weren't ready for. Please forgive me. And if you're never ready to re-marry, I shall accept your decision. I only ask that we remain friends, that I may share your company."

Friends?

Had he been nipping the brandy already?

Friends didn't do the naughty, wonderful things

she yearned to do with him.

"Oh, Griffin. I was looking for you to beg you to forgive me for hurting you. I was wrong. So, so wrong. I love you too. I truly, truly do. I want to be with you more than anything else."

Touching his dear face, she blinked through the joyful moisture blurring her vision.

"It would be the greatest privilege to be your wife." An impulse sprang to mind, and she clasped his hand. "Will you marry me?"

Chuckling delightedly, he crushed her to his chest.

"Yes. Yes! Lord, yes. I shall marry you, you delightfully unpredictable woman."

She tilted her head back, eyeing the kissing bough above their heads. "I believe a kiss is in order."

"Go on, man," Sutcliffe said. "Kiss her. I'm hungry, as are we all."

Everleigh spun around to find the corridor full of amused guests.

Dandridge, grinning ear to ear, pulled his wife to his side and dropped a quick peck on her temple. Ophelia and Gabriella hugged each other. Nicolette eyed Westfall with a considering look. Jessica, Rayne, and Theadosia beamed like they'd planned the whole affair.

Griffin cupped Everleigh's chin, gently drawing it upward.

"Happy Christmas, Everleigh."

And right there in front of everyone, Griffin, Duke of Sheffield, gave her a kiss that she nor he nor the other guests would soon forget.

Epilogue

2 September 1810
Rome, Italy

Everleigh chuckled and shook her head as Claire, her silken ears flapping, raced by in pursuit of the ball Sarah had thrown. Those two never grew tired of that game. The stately Italian villa they'd let for the next month boasted an enclosed courtyard perfect for energetic dogs and almost-four-year-olds.

"Mama, did you see Claire fetch the ball?"

Sarah bent to retrieve the slobbery orb.

"I did, darling." A feathery fluttering in her belly startled Everleigh. She cradled the small mound with both hands. "Well, hello there, precious. Do you hear your sister and Mama?"

The babe moved again.

"Griffin, the baby is moving! Here, you must feel."

She pressed his hand to her tummy. Another flicker caused her to giggle, and a goofy grin divided his face.

"Energetic little fellow, isn't he?" He bent low, murmuring to the small mound. "This is your papa, and he loves you very, very much."

"This is only the beginning." She ran her palms over her stomach. "Theadosia said she could see Amber's entire foot pressed against her belly at times."

His gaze fell on the simple gold band encircling her ring finger. "I wish you'd let me buy you a proper wedding ring, sweet."

She held her hand up, admiring the simple ring. "Not a bit of it. I found this in my Christmas pudding after asking you to marry me. It's perfect. It was meant to be."

Actually, nearly everybody found a ring that

evening, thanks to Griffin's sweet-talking the cook. Not everyone was as pleased as Everleigh had been to discover the trinket.

Wrapping an arm around her shoulders, he drew her near. "You forget, I asked you first."

"Yes, but I turned you down, so it was only fitting that I propose to you, scandalous though it was."

"How about an emerald ring you could wear with this band then?" He caressed her fingers.

"I suppose, if you insist," she teased.

He knew her weakness for emeralds.

She rested her head against his chest. Married for seven months already. Their wedding trip had been delayed due to Caroline Chatterton's devious machinations. Somehow, she'd persuaded the local magistrate to open an inquiry into Frederick's and Arnold's deaths.

Probably by bedding the dumpling of a man.

Everleigh hadn't been permitted to leave the country during the investigation, which, after five months, completely exonerated her. Caroline, the fool, hadn't been as fortunate. Seems she'd been cuckolding

Frederick with a not-altogether-too-bright fellow of questionable repute, who had taken her at her word when she said she wished her husband and father-in-law were dead. The fellow had confessed that she'd wanted Everleigh dead, but he didn't hold with killing women.

Ironically, Caroline—fortunate to have escaped the hangman's noose—now sailed for the same penal colony Theadosia's father pastored. Her former lover hadn't been as fortunate.

The postponed honeymoon had worked out well in the end. Everleigh had been able to attend Jessica's and Nicolette's weddings, as well as the dowager duchess of Sutcliffe's marriage to Jerome DuBoise.

Griffin was convinced he'd orchestrated that union, but the Duke of Sutcliffe claimed he'd been responsible.

Sarah paused in her romps to trot over to her new governess, Miss Brimble. Nurse had gratefully retired to a comfortable cottage in Bristol, and Miss Brimble, being several generations younger and the oldest of twelve siblings, proved skilled at managing Sarah.

Maya and Jenny—the name Sarah picked for the doll Everleigh made her—sat serenely on the tolerant governess's lap.

"Let's go for a walk, my dears." Miss Brimble stood, and Sarah gathered her dollies in her arms.

Claire, tongue lolling, had plopped herself at Miss Brimble's feet, but the instant the governess stood, the spaniel leaped to all fours.

"Miss Sarah, shall we explore the maze?" The governess looked to Everleigh for approval and after receiving a nod, asked, "Shall I hold one of your babies for you?"

Sarah tilted her head and extended both before her, considering them. She passed Miss Brimble Jenny. "Maya needs extra 'tention, so she doesn't get jealous of Jenny."

Was that a hint?

Sarah had been ecstatic when Everleigh and Griffin had told her she would soon be a big sister. Her enthusiasm waned considerably when she learned she might have a little brother, and a jot more when told she couldn't dress the new baby in her dollies' clothes.

As Sarah and Miss Brimble disappeared into the labyrinth, Everleigh turned into Griffin's embrace and hugged him.

"I never thought I could be this happy, Griffin. I love you so much, it almost hurts sometimes." She tilted her head into the crook of his shoulder. "Tell me again when you knew you loved me. I never tire of hearing it."

He pressed a tender kiss to her forehead.

"I knew the moment you scooped Sarah into your arms in the drawing room, and my heart stood still for an instant, that I'd found the woman I was meant to spend the rest of my life with."

About the Author

USA Today Bestselling, award-winning author COLLETTE CAMERON® scribbles Scottish and Regency historicals featuring dashing rogues and scoundrels and the intrepid damsels who reform them. Blessed with an overactive and witty muse that won't stop whispering new romantic romps in her ear, she's lived in Oregon her entire life, though she dreams of living in Scotland part-time. A self-confessed Cadbury chocoholic, you'll always find a dash of inspiration and a pinch of humor in her sweet-to-spicy timeless romances®.

Explore **Collette's worlds** at
www.collettecameron.com!

Join her **VIP Reader Club** and **FREE newsletter**.
Giggles guaranteed!

FREE BOOK: Join Collette's The Regency Rose®
VIP Reader Club to get updates on book releases,
cover reveals, contests and giveaways she reserves
exclusively for email and newsletter followers. Also,
any deals, sales, or special promotions are offered to
club members first. She will not share your name or
email, nor will she spam you.

http://bit.ly/TheRegencyRoseGift

Dearest Reader,

A DECEMBER WITH A DUKE is my 25th story and the third book in my Seductive Scoundrels Series. I wanted to create a quick read, a Christmas tale full of Regency Era yuletide traditions for my readers to escape the hustle and bustle that goes with the holiday season.

Griffin and Everleigh met in ONLY A DUKE WOULD DARE, but that encounter didn't go well. Now they are forced together at a month-long holiday house party, snowed in part of the time. Griffin set his mind to winning and healing Everleigh's wounded heart, and I think he did an admirable job.

I hope you think so too!

Please consider telling other readers why you enjoyed this book by reviewing it. I adore hearing from my readers.

So, with that, I'll leave you.

Here's wishing you many happy hours of reading, more happily-ever-afters than you can possibly enjoy in a lifetime, and abundant blessings to you and your loved ones.

Collette Cameron

A Diamond for a Duke

Seductive Scoundrels Book One

**A dour duke and a wistful wallflower—an
impossible match until fate intervenes.**

Jules, Sixth Duke of Dandridge disdains Society and
all its trappings, preferring the country's solitude and
peace. Already jaded after the woman he loved died
years ago, he's become even more so since
unexpectedly inheriting a dukedom's responsibilities
and finding himself the target of every husband-
hunting vixen in London.

Jemmah Dament has adored Jules from afar for
years—since before her family's financial and social
reversals. She dares not dream she can win a duke's
heart any more than she hopes to escape the life of
servitude imposed on her by an uncaring mother.
Jemmah knows full well Jules is too far above her
station now. Besides, his family has already selected

his perfect duchess: a poised, polished, exquisite blueblood.

A chance encounter reunites Jules and Jemmah, resulting in a passionate interlude neither can forget. Jules realizes he wants more—much more—than Jemmah's sweet kisses or her warming his bed. He must somehow convince her to gamble on a dour duke. But can Jemmah trust a man promised to another? One who's sworn never to love again?

Only a Duke Would Dare

Seductive Scoundrels, Book Two

"Delightful, dazzling, and oh-so delicious." ~Cheryl Bolen, **NYT** *Bestselling Author*

Faced with an impossible choice, could you devastate someone you love?

Caution: This book contains a philandering hero with a heart of gold, a fearless heroine adamant she'll decide her own destiny, a passel of roguish dukes and the daring damsels determined not to be seduced by them, and unforeseen twists that will keep you turning page after page.

Marriage—an unpleasant obligation

A troublesome addendum to his father's will requires Victor, Duke of Sutcliffe to marry before his twenty-seventh birthday. That doesn't mean he intends to alter his pleasure-seeking lifestyle. Mere weeks before he must wed, he ventures home, intent on finding the most biddable, forgettable miss in all of Essex. Except the first woman he encounters stirs far more than his interest, and Theadosia Brentwood is anything but unremarkable or dowdy.

Marriage—an impossible choice

Against her better judgement, and despite her father promising her hand to a man she detests, Theadosia clandestinely meets with Victor. Though she's far beneath his station and aware he must marry soon, she can't deny her growing fascination. When Victor unexpectedly proposes, Thea must make an unbearable decision—refuse to marry her father's pick and elope with Victor, who wouldn't wed at all except to save his fortune. If she does, her betrothed will reveal a scandalous secret, sending her father to prison and rendering her sister and mother homeless.

What Would a Duke Do?

Seductive Scoundrels, Book Four

He's bent on revenge. She's his enemy's granddaughter. He'll marry her...willing or not.

Maxwell, the Duke of Pennington, is a man focused on one thing: revenge. He'll stop at nothing to achieve his goal, including marrying the beautiful, unpredictable granddaughter of the man he seeks reprisal against— whether Gabriella is willing or not. As Max inexplicably finds himself drawn to the spirited minx, unforeseen doubts and guilt arise.

Miss Gabriella Breckensole is astonished when the enigmatic Duke of Pennington turns his romantic attentions on her. Debonair and confident, he set her heart fluttering from their first meeting. Far beneath his station, Gabby never hoped to win his favor, and she soon risks losing her heart to the roguish lord.

Until she accidentally overhears Maxwell vowing to

return her familial home to his dukedom and learns his courtship is a revenge-filled ploy. Even though he awakened feelings she never imagined possible, Gabriella now considers him an enemy. Can Max make the impossible choice between retribution or forever losing the only woman to ever touch his heart?

Excerpt

Enjoy the first chapter of

What Would A Duke Do?

Seductive Scoundrels, Book Four

Prologue

December 1809

Ridgewood Court, Essex England

Humming beneath her breath, Gabriella Breckensole practically skipped down the stairs on her way to meet the other female houseguests to make kissing boughs and other festive decorations. The past few days had been a whirlwind of activity, as her hostess, Theadosia, the Duchess of Sutcliffe, and one of her dearest friends, hosted a Christmastide house party, the likes of which Essex had never witnessed before.

The event was made all that much more enjoyable by the presence of Maxwell Woolbright, the Duke of Pennington. Since Gabriella and her twin sister had returned from finishing school almost two years ago, she'd encountered him at a few gatherings. He was quite the most dashing man she'd ever met, and despite being far above her station, she thrilled whenever he directed his attention her way.

Descending the last riser, she puzzled for a moment. Where were the ladies to meet? The drawing room, the floral salon, or the dining room? Forehead scrunched, she pulled her mouth to the side and started toward the drawing room. Halfway there, she remembered they were to meet in the slightly larger dining room. She spun around and marched in the other direction, passing the impressive library, its door slightly ajar.

"Harold Breckensole will pay for what he's done," a man declared in an angry, gruff voice.

Gabriella halted mid-step, her stomach plunging to her slippered feet. She swiftly looked up and down the vacant corridor before tip-toeing to the cracked doorway. Who spoke about her grandfather with such hostility?

Breath held, she peeked through the narrow opening. The Dukes of Sutcliffe, Pennington, and Sheffield stood beside the fireplace, facing each other.

Pennington held a glass of umber-colored spirits in one hand as he stared morosely into the capering flames. "I shall reclaim Hartfordshire Court. I swear."

"You say the estate was once part of the unentailed part of the duchy?" Sutcliffe asked, concern forming a line between his eyebrows.

Pennington tossed back a swallow of his drink. "Yes. It belonged to my grandmother's family for generations, and after what I've recently learned, I mean to see it restored to the ducal holdings, come hell or high water. And I'll destroy Breckensole too."

Slapping a hand over her mouth, she backed away, shaking her head as stinging tears slid from the corners of her eyes.

Oh, my stars.

She'd been halfway to falling in love with a man bent on revenge of some sort. Gabriella jutted her chin up, angrily swiping at her cheeks. The Duke of Pennington had just become her enemy.

1

Late March 1810

Colechester, Essex, England

"**M**iss Breckensole, what an unexpected...pleasure," a man drawled in a cultured voice, the merest hint of laughter coloring his melodious baritone.

Unexpected and wholly unwelcome.

Gabriella froze in admiration for Nicolette Twistleton's adorable pug puppy and barely refrained from gnashing her teeth. She knew full well who stood behind her. The odious, arrogant—*annoying as Hades*—Maxwell, Duke of Pennington. His delicious cologne wafted past her nostrils, and she let her eyelids drift half shut as she ordered her heart to resume its regular cadence.

He didn't know what she'd discovered about him. That he was a dishonorable, deceiving blackguard behind his oh, so charming demeanor. And he meant to destroy her grandfather. That knowledge bolstered her courage and settled her erratic pulse.

One midnight eyebrow arched questioningly; Nicolette threw her a harried glance before dipping into a curtsy. "Your Grace."

Gabriella hadn't confided in Nicolette. Hadn't confided in anyone as to why she disliked him so very much. Quashing her irritation at his appearance and his daring to greet her as if they were the greatest of friends, she schooled her features into blandness before turning and sinking into the expected deferential greeting. "Duke."

He bowed; his strong mouth slanted into his usual half-mocking smile.

"What brings you to town?" He glanced around. "Your sister or grandmother aren't with you? Or an abigail either?" A hint of disapproval edged his observation. "Did you come with Miss Twistleton?"

Beast. Who was he to question her conduct? She wasn't accountable to him.

"No, I am here with my mother." Nicolette cast Gabriella another bewildered glance. "She's in the milliner's."

Surely, he was aware, as was the whole of Colechester, that a lady's maid was an unnecessary expense, according to Gabriella's grandfather. That the duke so offhandedly and publicly made mention of the deficiency angered and chagrined her.

Pennington turned an expectant look upon her. As if he were entitled to have an answer because, after all, *he* was the much sought-after Duke of Pennington.

Edging her chin upward, Gabriella clutched her packages tighter, one of which was her twin's birthday present. She saved for months to be able to surprise Ophelia with the mazarine blue velvet cloak.

"Grandmama is unwell, and Ophelia stayed home to care for her." She wouldn't offer him further explanation.

"I am truly sorry to hear that. May I have my physician call upon her?" he asked, all solicitousness, even going so far as to lower his brows as if he truly cared. A concern she knew to be feigned given what she'd overheard at the Duke and Duchess of Sutcliffe's Christmastide house party last December.

"That's not necessary. She was seen by one only last week." My, she sounded positively unaffected. The epitome of a self-possessed gently-bred young woman.

Inside, she fumed at his forwardness.

How she wanted to rail at him. To tell him precisely what she thought of his nefarious scheme. Why did he—*conceited, handsome rakehell*—have to be in Colechester today too? He promptly turned her much-anticipated afternoon outing sour. Freshly cut lemon or gooseberry face-puckering, attitude-ruining sour.

And why he insisted upon trying to speak to her at every opportunity, she couldn't conceive. Three months ago, and the few unfortunate occasions they'd come across each other since she'd made her feelings perfectly clear—to-the-point-of-rudeness-clear.

She'd heard him vow to the Dukes of Sheffield and Sutcliffe that *come hell or high water*— Pennington's very sternly muttered words—he'd reclaim the lands that had once been an unentailed part of the duchy. Lands that had belonged to his grandmother's family for generations.

Property, which included her beloved home, Hartfordshire Court. A holding that Grandpapa had purchased, fair and square, from the duke's own degenerate grandfather decades before and which, with hard work and industry, had made the estate prosperous.

"Mama is so pleased you are to attend our musical assembly, Your Grace," Nicolette blurted. As if sensing the stilted silence and not understanding the reason why, but wanting to defuse the tangible awkwardness.

Unable to contain her disbelief, Gabriella sent him a quick glance from beneath her lashes.

He was to attend? *Of all the dashed rotten luck.*

He rarely remained at his country seat past mid-

March. London held far more appeal to a man of the world like him, and truth be told, she had anticipated—*needed*—a few months' reprieve from his presence.

She and Ophelia were to attend as well, but now she no longer anticipated her first social foray other than tea in two months as she had a minute ago.

Nicolette shifted the puppy and received a wet tongue on the cheek for her efforts.

"No licking, Bella," she admonished while rubbing the pup behind her ears. "It's also Gabriella's birthday that day," she offered with an impish twinkle in her eye. "She'll be one and twenty."

Gabriella shot her a quelling glance. The world—*he*—didn't need to know she was practically on the shelf with no prospects, save spinsterhood.

"I quite look forward to the entertainment." Insincerity rang in his tone as he gave a gracious nod and continued staring at Gabriella. "And also, to wish you a happy day, Miss Breckensole." The latter held a note of authenticity. He flicked his gaze down the street, seeming uncharacteristically uncertain. "Ladies, would you join me for a cup of chocolate or coffee?"

The Prince's Coffee House was four doors down and acclaimed not only for its hot beverages but also its ambiance and scrumptious pastries. Not that Gabriella had ever sampled either.

She'd wanted to, but Grandpapa frowned upon eating in the village. A waste of good coin, he grumbled.

Nicolette shook her head, no genuine regret shadowing her face. After being jilted, she bore disdain for every male, save her brother, the Earl of Scarborough. "I fear Mama is expecting me inside. I only came outside for Bella's sake."

"And I must return home straightaway." Gabriella signaled her driver with a flick of her wrist and slant of her head. She'd finished her shopping before bumping into Nicolette and the newest addition to the Twistleton household.

Amid a chorus of creaks and groans, her grandfather's slightly lopsided and dated coach pulled alongside her. Jackson, the groomsman, climbed down and after three rigorous attempts, managed to lower the steps. She passed him her parcels, which he promptly placed inside the conveyance.

"Please allow me." The duke stepped forward and offered his hand to assist her inside.

While she wanted to give him the cut by refusing to accept his offer, Nicolette was sure to interrogate her as to why she'd been so rude the next time they met. A year ago, even three months ago, Gabriella would've been overjoyed at his attention. Now, he was her enemy. A handsome, dangerous, cunning, and unpredictable nemesis.

She placed her fingertips atop his palm as lightly as she could and entered the rickety out-of-fashion forty-year-old coach. Lips melded, she studiously disregarded the alarming jolt of sensation zipping up her arm at his touch. She should feel nothing but contempt for him and most assuredly entertain no attraction.

The duke didn't immediately close the door behind her. His gaze probed hers for a long sliver of a moment, and suddenly the coach became very confining. And hot. She waved her hand before her face, having left her fan at home. "Might I call upon you tomorrow?"

Is he utterly daft?

"Perhaps we might take a ride? Naturally, Miss Ophelia is welcome too."

That latter seemed more of an after-thought. He knew she couldn't ride out alone with him, and he was mad as a Bedlam guest if he truly believed she'd willingly spend time in his company.

Gabriella met his gaze straight on. Something undefinable shadowed the depths of his unusual eyes— one green and one blue. "I must decline, Your Grace. Once again, I also must ask you to direct your attention elsewhere. I am not now, nor will I ever be, receptive to them."

If she never spoke to him again, it would be too soon.

Did he really think that just because he was a duke and she was the lowly granddaughter of a gentleman-farmer, she'd jump at the opportunity to spend time in his company?

You did at one time. And suffered a broken heart when his true character became evident.

Not. Anymore. Never again. Not when she knew his true motivation for seeking her company. How much her feelings had changed for him these past months.

At once his striking countenance grew shuttered, his high cheekbones more pronounced with... Anger? Disappointment? "We shall see, *chérie*. We shall see."

"What, precisely, do you mean by that?" Something very near dread clogged her throat, and the words came out husky rather than terse as she'd intended.

Instead of answering, he offered an enigmatic smile and doffed his hat, the afternoon sunlight glinting on his raven hair. "Good day."

We shall see, chérie. We shall see.

His words replaying over and over in her mind, she remained immobile, her focus trained on his retreating form until he disappeared into the Pony and Pint instead of The Prince's Coffee House. At one time, she'd fancied herself enamored of him. She'd been flattered he'd turned his ducal attention on her: a simple country girl without prospects.

Firmly stifling those memories and the associated emotions, she tapped the roof. "Home. Jackson, and do hurry. Grandmama needs her medicines."

And I need to put distance between myself and the Duke of Pennington.

Because even though Gabriella knew the truth, a tiny part of her heart ached for him, and she loathed herself for that weakness.

~*~

Two hours later, shivering and briskly rubbing her arms, Gabriella bent forward to peer out the coach window again.

Tentatively probing her head, she winced. The knot from smacking her noggin on the side of the vehicle when the axle snapped hadn't grown any larger. Neither did it bleed. Nonetheless, the walnut-sized lump ached with the ferocity of a newly trapped tiger. A superbly large, sharp-toothed, and foul-tempered beast.

"Really," she muttered, exasperated and

uncharacteristically cross from hunger, cold, and the painful bump. "Whatever can be taking Jackson so long to return? Hartsfordshire Court isn't so very blasted far."

Less than two miles, she estimated after another glance at the familiar green meadow sloping to the winding river beyond. The recent rains caused the brown-tinged water to run high and spill over its banks, as it did nearly every spring. In the summer, the lush grasslands fed Grandpapa's famed South Devon cattle on one side and their neighbor, the Duke of Pennington's fluffy black-faced sheep on the other.

An uncharitable thought about the distinction between the keen intelligence of cows and sheep's lack of acumen tried to form, but she squelched it. It wasn't the poor sheep's fault she couldn't abide their owner.

After repeatedly assuring her hesitant coachman that she would be perfectly fine until he returned with the seldom-used phaeton, Jackson had swiftly stridden away. Not, however, without turning to work his worried gaze over her, the team, and the disabled coach's crippled wheel thrice. Each time, she donned a smile wide enough to crack her cheeks and made a shooing motion for him to continue on.

For pity's sake. Gabriella wasn't one of those silly, simpering misses afraid the hem of her skirt might become dusty or who shrieked hysterically upon a cobweb brushing her gloves or cheek. So long as the eight-fuzzy-legged spider had *long* since removed itself to a new home.

If it weren't for her impractical footwear, Gabriella would've walked as well. But, she'd no wish for bruised feet or the lecture certain to follow from dear Grandpapa about the cost of replacing ruined slippers. And that would probably produce another discourse about unnecessary trips to Colechester for what he deemed nonsensical fripperies.

Perhaps they were absurd to a man given to wearing the same staid suit and shoes for the past five years as Grandpapa had been. But Ophelia's birthday present wasn't a silly frippery. Neither were Grandmama's medicine nor the chemises for Gabriella and her sister frivolous expenses. It had been three years since anyone had purchased new undergarments.

With her leftover pin money—one half a crown every month—Gabriella had purchased the beloved hunch-shouldered curmudgeon his favorite blend of pipe tobacco. Oh, he'd grumble and grouse over the wasteful spending, but she hadn't a doubt she'd earn a kiss upon her forehead before he shuffled off to enjoy a pipe and a tot in his fusty study amongst his even fustier tomes.

A wry smile quirked her mouth.

Did Grandpapa use the same tobacco five times as he insisted Grandmama do with tea leaves? Anything to save a penny or two. The Breckensoles didn't enjoy neat lumps of white sugar in their tea either, but rather the golden-brown nubs chiseled from a cheaper hard-as-a-blasted-boulder loaf. Since they never—truly never—had guests for tea or for any other occasion for that matter, there was no need to feel a trifle embarrassed at the economy.

She ran a gloved finger over the lumpy parcel containing the umber-brown bottles for her grandmother. A month ago, a nasty cough had settled in Grandmama's lungs, and she couldn't shake the ailment.

Gabriella's current discomfort tugged her meandering musings back to her immediate situation. For all of two seconds—fine, mayhap three—she'd considered riding one of the horses still harnessed to the coach home. But that would've required hiking her gown knee-high and riding astride. Even she daren't that degree of boldness.

Nonetheless, on days she yearned to toss aside Society's and her strict grandparents' constraints, she *might've* been known to sneak a horse from the stables and ride along the river: bonnet-free and skirts rucked most inappropriately high. Oh, the freedom was wondrous, though the tell-tale freckles that were wont to sprout upon her nose usually gave her recklessness away.

Her grandparents never lectured, but their silent disapproval was sufficient to quell her hoydenish ways. For a week or two.

The carriage made an eerie noise, the way a vehicle sounded in the throes of death. *If* a vehicle were capable of such a thing. Another juddering crack followed as the damaged side wedged deeper into the dirt.

She let loose a softly-sworn oath no respectable woman ought to know, let alone utter aloud as she grabbed the seat to keep from tumbling onto the floor. A labored groan and a piercing creak followed on the heels of her crude vulgarity, and a five-inch-long jagged crack split the near window.

"Confound it."

A new chill skidded down her spine as she mentally braced herself for Grandpapa's intense displeasure. He'd be aggravated about the damage to the coach, but more so about the cost to repair it. A frugal, self-made man, he was as reluctant to part with a coin as he was to leave Hartfordshire Court. Others who didn't know him well called him stingy and miserly.

In the fifteen years since coming to live at Hartfordshire, Gabriella could count on two hands the number of times either grandparent had left the estate. She would shrivel up and die if forced to stay there for months.

Yet, her hermit-like grandparents had been diligent in assuring she and her sister never lacked for company or social interactions. They'd even conceded to send the twins to finishing school. At no little cost either. What a juxtaposition. Her grandparents eschewed all things social, but she and her sister craved the routs, soirees, balls, picnics, musical parties, and all else that guaranteed a superior assemblage.

One troublesome, unignorable fact remained unaddressed, however. Grandpapa had never spoken of a dowry for either of them. They'd never wanted for necessities, but Gabriella suspected his pockets weren't as flush as he'd have his family believe.

Her heart gave a queer pang. It wasn't exactly worry or distress. But neither was the peculiar feeling frustration or disappointment. Nevertheless, it left her unsettled. Discontent and restless. Disconcerted about what her future might entail. Ophelia's too.

As improbable as it was, except for splurging on the matched team and phaeton, her grandfather had been less inclined to spend money after the twins returned home two years ago. Now, almost one and twenty, their aging grandparents' health beginning to fail, and their neighbor, the mercenary Duke of Pennington, bent on stealing Hartsfordshire Court from them, Gabriella fretted about what would happen to her sister if neither one of them married and soon.

There weren't exactly men—noble or otherwise—scurrying to form a queue to court either of them. Or to dance with them at assemblies or request romantic strolls through opulent gardens. No posies, sweets, or poems regularly found their way to the house's front door. On *any* basis, for that matter.

Oh, the country gentlemen were kind and polite enough. Indeed, some aristocrats and gentry—even a rogue or two—had been downright charming and flirtatious. More than one had hinted they'd like to pursue an immoral liaison. But the simple truth was as obvious as a giraffe's purple tongue sampling pea soup in the dining room. Dowerless, Gabriella's and Ophelia's prospects were few.

Nonexistent, truth to tell.

For one horrid, ugly fact couldn't be overlooked: a woman without a dowry, no matter how refined, immaculately fitted out, or proficient in French, Latin, Spanish, painting, playing the pianoforte—or the violin in Gabriella's case—and managing a household she might be, without the lure of a marriage settlement to entice a respectable suitor, such an unfortunate lady was labeled an undesirable.

And much like other hapless women in the same ill-fated predicament, spinsterhood, dark and foreboding, loomed on the horizon, a slightly terrifying fate for any young woman.

Which made the duke's interest in her all the more questionable. He couldn't possibly have honorable intentions.

She pursed her mouth, drawing her eyebrows into a taut line. Barbaric, this business of bribing a man with money, land, and the good Lord only knew what else to take a woman to wife. Why couldn't love be enough?

Like Theadosia and Sutcliffe? Or her maternal cousin Everleigh and the Duke of Sheffield? Or even Jemmah and Jules, the Duke and Duchess of Dandridge? Once not so long ago, Gabriella had yearned for that kind of love. Had dared to hope she might've found it, but the object of her affections had turned out to be a colossal rat.

Unfortunately, such was the nature of the Marriage Mart. Without dowries, Gabriella and her twin could look forward to caring for their grandparents into their dotage rather than marry and have families. Their lack of suitors could be laid at Society's silk-clad feet. Strictures, along with a goodly portion of greed and hunger for power, dictated most matches. That, regrettably, was an indisputable fact.

Something uncomfortable and slightly terrifying, much like melancholy, turned over in her breast and swirled in her stomach. To distract herself from her somber reflections, she inspected the lonely road once more.

The fading afternoon sun filtering through the towering evergreen treetops on the other side of the deserted track confirmed dusk's dark cloak and chill would blanket the countryside soon. For at least the sixth time in the past hour, Gabriella examined the dainty timepiece pinned to her spencer.

She frowned and gave it a little shake. Was the deuced thing working?

Yes, the big hand shifted just then. She huffed out a small petulant sigh, for she recognized her own impatience.

Where the devil was Jackson, for pity's sake? Had something waylaid him? *Obviously.* Yes, but what? The unbidden thoughts agitated her already heightened nerves. Nerves that had been fraught since departing the village earlier.

Angered anew at Pennington's audacity, she pressed her lips into an irritated line and fisted her hands. Only he could make her so peeved.

Bloody, greedy bounder. By Jove, didn't he have enough? Why must he covet what we have too?

Chartworth Hall was an immense estate boasting some two-thousand acres, a mansion—more castle than a house—a hunting lodge, a dower house, embarrassingly massive and full stables, and numerous other outbuildings.

Why the duke focused on Hartfordshire's acres and seventeen-room residence, quite desperately in need of refurbishing and restoration, made no sense. She didn't know the particulars of the sale. Neither did she understand how the unentailed property came to be adjacent to the entailed lands, but she didn't give a fig.

What she *did* care about was the duke's callousness. His insensitivity and cold-heartedness. He hadn't a thought for any of the Breckensoles, of displacing them from their home. Oh, no. His only concern was how to cheat Grandpapa out of his property and to expand the already enormous ducal holdings.

By thunder, she wouldn't permit it. She would not.

Printed in Great Britain
by Amazon

17831555R00119